9/15/75 ret'd written →
on pg.

D0056526

Damage Noted

"*What, girls in racing?*" Henry ___,
trainer of the Black Stallion, exploded
at the thought of girls competing against
men in the sport he loved.

"They're dynamite," he warned.
"Just because of their sex they create
problems we wouldn't have otherwise.
They get emotionally involved with
their horses, everything. Racing is a
rough business; it's not for girls."

Alec Ramsay, rider of the Black Stallion, had been taught to have respect for
Henry's authority. Yet he found that he
could not agree with Henry simply because the old man expected him to do
so. One day, in desperate need of help
at Hopeful Farm, Alec hired a girl
named Pam to work for them. Little did
he dream that she would be the catalyst
who would rock his own world as well
as Henry's and deeply involve the Black
Stallion.

Here is a timely story of girls in today's racing scene—from stock farm to
race track, from mucking out stalls in
the morning to wearing racing silks in
the afternoon. It is also a story of two
young people, Pam and Alec, who belong to two different worlds—one of
trust and the other of cynicism—brought
together by their great love for horses.

Many readers of the famous Black
Stallion series have long awaited this
book, for in it a young girl enters the life
of Alec Ramsay.

BLACK STALLION

FLAME

SATAN

BLACK MINX

BONFIRE

The
Black Stallion
and the Girl

Other books by
Walter Farley
The Black Stallion
The Black Stallion Returns
Son of the Black Stallion
The Island Stallion
The Black Stallion and Satan
The Blood Bay Colt
The Island Stallion's Fury
The Black Stallion's Filly
The Black Stallion Revolts
The Black Stallion's Sulky Colt
The Island Stallion Races
The Black Stallion's Courage
The Black Stallion Mystery
The Horse Tamer
The Black Stallion and Flame
The Black Stallion Challenged
The Black Stallion's Ghost
Man O' War
The Great Dane Thor

And for
Younger Readers
Big Black Horse
Little Black, a Pony
Little Black Goes to the Circus
The Horse That Swam Away
The Little Black Pony Races

The
Black Stallion
and the Girl

BY WALTER FARLEY

Illustrated by Angie Draper

RANDOM HOUSE   NEW YORK

X A

Copyright © 1971 by Walter Farley

All rights reserved under International and Pan-American Copyright Conventions. Published in the United States by Random House, Inc., New York, and simultaneously in Canada by Random House of Canada Limited, Toronto.

Trade Edition: ISBN: 0-394-82145-9
Library Edition: ISBN: 0-394-92145-3
Library of Congress Catalog Card Number: 75-147884

Manufactured in the United States of America

SAN RAFAEL, PUBLIC LIBRARY
SAN RAFAEL, CALIFORNIA
63765

For
Alice and Steve and Tim

SAPSIS 11/7. 4.50

Contents

The
Black Stallion
and the Girl

1 • *Help Wanted, Hopeful Farm*

It was shortly after dawn when Alec Ramsay walked into the training barn at Hopeful Farm and found the new employee man-handling Black Sand. He ran into the stall and caught the man's foot as it swung hard toward Black Sand's belly. Once he had hold of it, Alec heaved backward, upsetting the man and putting him down in the straw.

"I told you never to rough up these colts," Alec shouted angrily. "Now get out of here."

The man lay still, his jaws and eyes open, breathing heavily. "That crazy colt bit me," he said. His fingers tightened about the bridle in his hands as if he were about to swing it at Black Sand's head.

Alec moved the colt back, knowing the ex-jockey had been drinking and it would not be easy to get rid of him.

"That's still no reason to hit him," Alec said. "You're through."

The man attempted to get up, the big muscles of his shoulders bunching. "Give me another chance, Alec," he pleaded. "It won't happen again."

Alec didn't believe him. The tone of his voice was all wrong, just as his apology was meaningless. "I hired you knowing you drank," Alec said. "You knew I knew. You promised it wouldn't happen here. I said I'd give you one chance, but only one, because nobody else in the business would hire you."

"I know," the man said, his voice surly. "You don't have to give me any rundown."

"Then you know why I'm not giving you another chance," Alec said. "Get up. I'll make out your check and you can get out of here."

The man raised a hand, big and rough and grimy, asking for Alec's help in rising. He seemed unsteady; as if he couldn't make it alone.

Alec hesitated before reaching out. The ex-jockey was in his mid-forties, no taller than he but more heavily built in the shoulders and with all the strength that came from many years of racing horses. Alec decided he had to take a chance; he had to get him out of the stall where he could do no harm to the colt.

4

The man was in a half-crouch when their hands met. Without any warning, he swung the bridle hard. Alec deflected the steel bit but the leather reins lashed his face. Then the man's hurtling body was on top of him, hands tearing at his eyes and head. As Alec fell, he managed to swing a booted foot, catching his opponent in the knees and sending him sprawling beside him. He rolled over and chopped hard at the man's throat with the side of his hand.

The man gasped for breath, but he straightened and swung violently upward, with Alec clinging to his back. They went reeling backward to fall in the straw with Alec on the bottom.

Alec twisted, avoiding the man's elbows, which sought to batter his head and face; then he got in several swift punches of his own that knocked his opponent off him. Quickly, he scrambled to his feet and struck at the man's right wrist with the side of his hand. There was a cry of pain as the man fell back gasping, his wrist dangling brokenly.

"Enough," he whimpered.

Alec shoved him out of the stall and followed him to the apartment on the second floor of the barn. It was a mess with empty wine and liquor bottles everywhere, dirty dishes and glasses piled high, soiled clothes and bed linen—and the man had occupied it less than a week.

"Pack up," Alec said. "I'll wait and take you to the hospital. You need help for more than your wrist."

"Not me, you won't," the ex-jockey said. "You're not

takin' me to no hospital. Just give me my check and I'll get out of here."

Later, with the man gone, Alec returned to his office and read the advertisement he had been running in all horse publications for the past six months.

WANTED: Reliable man for stable on race-horse farm. Must have professional experience handling and riding young horses. Must be of good character. Must provide references. Good wages with furnished apartment and fringe benefits. Write Hopeful Farm, Box 37, Millville, N. Y.

The advertisement had not been very successful. Alec had hired several men for the job but none had been reliable. Good help was hard to get and even more difficult to keep.

Hopeful Farm was an incorporated business with his parents and Henry Dailey, the trainer, as the principal stockholders. Officially, his own position was that of stable rider, since one could not own and ride a race horse. However, while his parents lived on the farm and his father was responsible for the hiring of local help for maintenance work, Alec was in charge of finding the professional horseman to break and school the two-year-olds. He couldn't handle the colts himself, for he and Henry Dailey had begun a long summer of racing their great champion, the Black Stallion, in New York City. But

6

occasionally Alec got a few days off and returned home, helping his father supervise the tremendous amount of work involved in running the farm.

Frustrated and impatient, Alec went to the window that overlooked the separate paddocks where the two-year-olds were grazing and playing on the best grass that could be grown. Black Sand was among them and clearly enjoying his freedom. If he could not get the man he needed, Alec decided, it would be far better to turn out the young stock until he and Henry had time to handle it.

Alec watched the horses. Some of them were unsteady on their legs, trying to find their balance, but they were all of a dazzling and powerful beauty. Their long, thick manes and fine coats—black, bay, chestnut and gray—had the gleam of wild silk in the early morning sun. Their deep shoulders and chests and muscular, arched necks breathed forth inexhaustible strength, endurance and spirit. They would be horses to reckon with on the race track, he knew. The future of Hopeful Farm rested on their young backs.

Beyond, in an adjacent field, grazed the heavy but loving mares with suckling foals at their sides. They, too, would help determine the future of Hopeful Farm.

Alec saw a car stop in the main driveway, which ran between the two fields. After a few minutes it moved forward again, only to stop once more, its driver apparently watching the horses. The car was an old model Chevrolet sedan with a torn right fender. Multi-colored

7

flowers were painted on its gray body. Finally, it turned toward the barn, disappearing from view.

Guests weren't welcome before nine o'clock and Alec regretted not having closed the main gate. The sign at the end of the driveway pointed the way to his office and he steeled himself for the unwelcome task of receiving a visitor so early. He would be courteous but brief, he decided; otherwise, he wouldn't be able to handle it, not on top of everything else.

The girl appeared in his open doorway and said, "Good Morning, Sun . . . I mean, sir." She corrected herself hastily but without embarrassment.

Alec was totally unprepared for a girl visitor. "*Son?*" he asked bewilderedly. The girl was certainly no older than he.

"Sun," she repeated, laughing. "*S . . . u . . . n*. It's crazy, I know, but I always say it in the morning, and people look at me just as startled as you do. I guess it's because I feel good when the sun is out. Some days better than others, and this is one of the best." She looked out the window. "They're beautiful horses, more beautiful than I ever expected and I expected a lot."

"And when the sun isn't out?" Alec asked, surprised that he was continuing such a conversation. Her eyes were a most uncommon blue and held a piercing liveliness.

"Oh, then I pretend it is. It can be done, you know, if you just put your mind to it. You believe it's there and it is. When I was little, my father used to hold me

8

up to the window, morning and night, sun or no sun, and he'd say, 'Good Morning, Sun' and 'Good night, Sun.' "

"Then you must always feel good," Alec said, "whether the sun's out or not."

"Not *always,* not *every* day, that's impossible," she said, laughing again. "But most of the time I do. Don't you?" she asked abruptly.

Alec found that he was strangely annoyed by her question. And the way she hadn't even waited for him to answer; she had just assumed that she knew what his answer would be.

"I came to apply for the job," she said seriously. "The one you've been advertising for months in *Blood Horse.* I hope you haven't filled it."

Alec's eyes changed; there was no longer any interest in them. He didn't want anyone like this for the job. He needed professional help. He was running no school for would-be riders and starry-eyed kids. Yet he heard himself ask, "What's your name?"

"Pam," she said.

There was a serenity in her eyes that he knew was a sharp contrast to the restlessness in his own, and she seemed aware of it. "And your last name?"

"Athena," she said, watching him without moving her eyes, without blinking.

"That's ridiculous," he said, louder than he meant to, thereby adding to his uneasiness. "Athena was some kind of a Greek goddess. It can't be your last name."

"Why not?" she asked. "There's nothing wrong with it, is there?" Her voice was very clear, even gentle. "Actually, Athena was a goddess who both protected the arts and went to battle in defense of them," she added in quiet explanation.

"If you say so," Alec said. She might well be of Grecian descent at that, he decided. The sunlight coming through the window shone on her with a violent light, accentuating her high, sharp cheekbones, her long-lashed blue eyes and her very tanned skin. Her blond hair was tied back in a long ponytail, exposing ears as small and delicately sculptured as her nose. She looked, despite her outspokenness, very vulnerable and sensitive.

"Do you want to know the rest?" she asked, moving away from the window to stand in front of him.

He realized only then how truly small she was. Her forehead barely came to his chest. "The rest of what?"

She laughed. "Well, why I feel I could fill the job. You see, I've been around horses all my life. I had my first pony almost before I could walk. Her name was Peek-a-Boo, a little chestnut Shetland mare with a long golden mane that covered her eyes. She used to peer at me through it, so I thought Peek-a-Boo was a good name for her. When she had her first foal, I was going to call him I-See-You but he turned out to be so fast that I named him Flash instead.

"Later, I was given my first horse. She was an Arabian mare and I named her Tena, short for Athena. I still have her and she's beautiful and a mother several times over. But when we were young together I'd ride her for miles and miles along the beach. She loved the sand and she'd lie in it, just like a person sunbathing. She loved swimming, too, and often we'd herd schools of fish that came close to shore. We'd move into them just like a cowboy herding cattle, cutting one group from another. It was lots of fun for us.

"That all happened in Florida, where my home is," she added quietly.

"Florida?" Alec repeated. "You're from Florida?"

"Yes, but I don't stay there much any more. It's as if an alarm clock goes off in my head, telling me it's time to leave and *do* things. There's not too much time, you know."

"Not too much time," Alec repeated. "For what?"

"For living, for being young like us," she replied, her candid eyes searching Alec's.

Alec ran a hand through his red hair and went back to his desk. He was finding it difficult to say what had to be said and for him this was very unusual. Ordinarily, he was capable of taking charge of most anything to which he set his hand and mind. He had trained himself to control his life.

"I really don't need you," he said abruptly. "I mean I'm in need of *professional* help. It's not that I want to be unkind, but I hear from so many young people like yourself."

"I suppose so," she said. "There must be thousands who'd like to work here and ride your horses."

"Hundreds, anyway," Alec answered. Her smile and eyes were making him uncomfortable again. "I can't do anything about hiring them."

"No, I suppose not. Horse-crazy kids just have to go it alone, scheming and dreaming. Professional horsemen like yourself can't take the time and responsibility to train them."

"Very few kids would stay with it," he said defensively. "It's hard and often dirty work, much more than they realize from books and movies. The time spent training them is lost. Few—if any—would remain."

"I know," she said. "I'd go, too, after a while; that is, even if you did hire me."

"You would?" Alec asked, surprised. "But you sounded so dedicated . . ."

"To horses, yes. I'll always love them and want to be around them, but there's that clock I told you about, the one in my head. You'll find it in the heads of lots of kids, if not in your own."

"I suppose so," he said.

"It doesn't mean I couldn't be of *temporary* help to you," she said quickly. "I've helped other professional horsemen, so maybe I'm more professional than you think. I've worked trotters and pacers at Ben White Raceway in Orlando, Florida, and ridden and jumped thoroughbreds all the way north to here. I could help you . . . I mean until you found your professional help."

In her face, Alec saw an unusual amount of strength

12

and eagerness. "I don't know," he said, realizing that if he hired her, even temporarily, Henry would be enraged. The old trainer had no use for girls around barns. He would see only her femininity, and her honest candor would infuriate him. And yet, if she could handle the horses, would it not give him the time he needed to find a reliable professional horseman?

Moments of uneasy silence passed for Alec. Her eyes, staring so intently into his, forced him to look deep into himself. He no longer thought *young*, he decided. He had become an old man before being a young one. He insisted upon professional help even though he'd begun as the rankest kind of an amateur himself. He spoke critically of would-be riders and starry-eyed kids, but he'd been one himself not so long ago. Had he completely forgotten what it was like to be young?

Alec met her gaze. Perhaps, if he made a sincere attempt to listen to her, he might learn what was going on with people his own age. It would be a welcome change.

"I'd like to see you ride," he said. "Then I'll decide."

2 ◆ *Black Sand*

Alec followed her into the corridor, but instead of going directly outside she stopped at Satan's stall. The first son of the Black Stallion was premier sire at Hopeful Farm while the Black was away racing. He had his head against the barred window of his stall, apparently watching the horses outside.

"I never thought I'd actually see him," she said, without turning to look at Alec. She was aware of nothing but the magnificent black horse. He was huge—so big, so powerful in chest and shoulders that in strength and beauty he surpassed anything she'd ever seen.

14

She called to him, her voice very low and gentle. Satan remained still, like a statue with the rays of the sun streaming upon it. A muscle quivered in his marvelously smooth skin, then another and still another. He was aware of her, and she spoke to him again.

Satan's chest swelled, his nostrils trembled; then he turned toward her, his eyes lighting up as he moved across the stall. He stood before the iron bars, eager for attention.

She reached into the stall and touched him, rubbing the white, diamond-shaped star in the center of his forehead.

Alec said, "He was a devil to break, but Henry Dailey, our trainer, worked on him as he will never work on another horse. Satan became a truly great horse, very competitive yet willing to obey the slightest hint of rein or leg. As far as Henry is concerned, Satan is the best we ever had."

"And for you?"

"No, not for me," he said quietly. "I have the Black."

The stallion's warm breath was caressing her hand. "You're both very lucky," she said, turning to him. "The most splendid gift of all is a noble horse. I suppose each of us chooses the horse he loves most for his own sake, not for the horse's sake. And each of us takes care of him not for the horse's sake but for his own."

Alec laughed at her unusual philosophy. "You mean we make our favorite horses what we are ourselves?" he asked

"Something like that," she replied. "Henry must demand unquestioned obedience, right?"

"He does."

"And you? What have you made of the Black?"

Alec smiled, enjoying her honest, straightforwardness. "I didn't make anything of him, really," he said. "I asked and he gave. I'd say the Black was more tamed than trained. It's always a little precarious when he's being handled."

"You mean there's always some danger involved?"

"Always," he said.

"And you wouldn't want it any other way," she said boldly. "Now I know you better."

She looked at him mischievously, and there were little quivers at the corners of her mouth. Finally, her smile broke through.

"I've known all along that girls have a reputation for loving horses and being passionately interested in learning about them," Alec said, "but I didn't know it included analyzing their riders and trainers as well."

She shrugged her shoulders. "Each of us does his own thing, whatever makes him most happy."

A few minutes later they walked along the paddock fences, their bodies lean and sharp, both wearing worn, blue Levis. Their eyes followed the two-year-old colts at play.

"Splendor in the morning sun!" she exclaimed. "And I'm sharing it with you, the most famous rider in all the land. It's hard to believe."

16

"Please," Alec said self-consciously, "if you're going to work here . . ."

"Am I?" she asked, turning to him. "If you hire me, I promise never to call you famous again."

"I'll decide when I see you ride."

"You'll be able to tell?"

"Yes. And that will be the end of it."

"Or the beginning," she said confidently. "Which horse?" she asked, turning back to the colts.

"Take your pick. They're all green-broke."

"My choice," she said, her gaze going to each paddock. It was difficult to decide and she took a long time. They were all so beautiful, so filled with their own strength and spirit and rivalry for each other.

With mounting impatience, Alec remarked, "You said that one selects a horse for his own sake, not for the horse's sake, so choose."

"There he is," she said, her answer quick and keen.

Black Sand was racing down his paddock toward them. He made a sweeping turn and ran by. "Yes, that's the one," Pam said eagerly, climbing the fence to sit on the top rail.

Alec said reluctantly, "It's a bad choice. He's the only one in the whole bunch I shouldn't let you ride. Pick another." He'd had enough trouble because of Black Sand for one day.

She turned back to the colt. He was dark brown, almost black, with a wide blaze running from forehead to nostrils and long white stockings on all four legs. "But

17

why?" she asked finally.

"He's the only one that hasn't been ridden in well over a month," Alec replied. "It wouldn't be fair to you. This is no contest, no challenge I'm asking of you. I only want to watch you ride a young horse."

Black Sand had come to a stop nearby, inquisitive and looking for attention. Sweat covered his flanks and he constantly tossed his head and whinnied.

"Is your concern for me or for the horse?" Pam asked.

"For you. He's by Satan, whose colts have his temperament, and the dam was an outside mare. His owner couldn't handle him."

The colt was close enough for Pam to see the deep scars running across his body. "From a whip?" she asked after a moment's silence.

Alec nodded. "Before we got him," he answered.

"I hope you lashed the owner as well."

"No, but we took him to court and got the colt away from him. That's more important."

"A man like that will probably never change," she said sadly, "but the horse will." She swung off the fence and caught the colt by the halter. Alec was stunned by her quickness, as Black Sand must have been.

There was no wickedness in the colt's deep-set eyes, only a settled rage—first a spark and then fire—at being held fast. He tried to rear but Pam kept him still.

"He is well where he should be well," she called to Alec. "If you let me ride him, it will be easy for you to de-

18

cide. You'll know one way or another in a matter of minutes."

Alec accepted her challenge, knowing she was right.
He felt that he could accurately predict the phases of the
coming battle. If she could handle Black Sand, he'd certainly hire her. It was more than the other men had been
able to do.

The colt snorted and Pam soothed him with a caress.
His nostrils were wide and flaring, his eyes surprised
and rebellious. He moved his big body against hers and
she scolded him. "I don't have to be strong to have the
courage to ride you. You belong to one who knows best
how to love you, that's all."

Alec came up and snapped a lead shank on the
halter ring. "Okay," he said quietly.

Together they took Black Sand from the paddock to
the training barn. They tacked him and he was so impatient to be off that he never stopped his dancing. Then
Alec led him back to the enclosed paddock. "Try him
here where he can't get away from you," he said.

Pam's eyes met those of the colt, so moist and brilliant. She passed her left hand over his near eye, closing
the lid, while stroking the muzzle with her other hand.
She began to hum softly, barely audible, but the colt
heard her.

Alec waited, no longer impatient; he knew what she
was attempting to do. The colt's ears stood high, turning
in her direction. She continued humming.

"Get back," she said finally, "I'll be all right now."

Alec hesitated, wanting to help her mount, but she persisted. "I don't need you. Please."

She removed her hand from the colt's eye and, suddenly, she was in the saddle, all in one swing, almost before Alec was aware of it. Every joint and muscle from ankle to neck had acted as one. Score one for her, Alec thought, and now . . .

The colt reared and Alec wondered what Pam would do about it. This bad habit accounted for the beatings Black Sand had taken from his former owner. There was always the danger of his going over backward and taking his rider with him.

She thwarted his first attempt by pressing forward with all her strength and weight against his withers until he came down. He went up again and this time she allowed him to reach his full height before moving her weight forward to stop him. He started down, but she flung her weight back again, the reins tight in her hands, holding him upright. His forelegs pawed the air with irregular, unordered force, trying to keep his balance beneath her shifting weight and hands.

He tried to go over backward but Pam threw her weight forward and released the reins. His hocks trembled beneath him. He lurched forward, trying to come down on his forelegs. She wouldn't let him, her weight and hands shifting back again as though determined to keep him on his hindlegs forever.

Alec realized then that Pam was not one to have an idea and let it lie idle; she did something about it quickly.

The contest went on for many minutes, with Alec watching the play of balances and counter-balances between horse and rider. What Pam was doing called for strength, skill, experience and instinct—perhaps instinct above all else. To keep the colt upright, she could not be a fraction of a second too late in correcting her hands and balance. She had to decide what he was about to do before he did it, and use her weight and strength as a counter-balance.

Henry had thrown the colt several times in an attempt to break him of rearing, but he'd never thought of keeping him up, reaching for the sky, until the colt was grateful to come down and, perhaps, stay down.

Pam straightened in her saddle, gripping the colt with her legs and holding him upright. His hocks trembled severely. She released him the moment he could not stand the strain any longer. She slackened the reins, loosened her knees, and hurled her weight forward.

"Go!" she called. In a mighty leap Black Sand had his forelegs down and was galloping.

His strides lengthened until he was approaching full speed, much too fast for so short and narrow a paddock. Alec expected him to run full tilt into the fence, if she didn't slow him down. It was much too high to jump.

Pam wasn't able to slow him down but, at the last moment, she swung hard in her saddle, laying her whole body against the colt's inner side. Then, with knees and hands, she turned him. His hurtling body was only inches from the fence, so that her outside leg was brushing against it. He flew along the fence and came racing back, the hammering of his hoofs shaking the earth.

She managed to stop his headlong rush not far from Alec. "He's marvelous!" she called, breathing heavily. "What's his name?"

"Black Sand," Alec replied, his eyes never leaving her. He realized what she had accomplished and shared her joy. She had a better seat and hands than anyone he'd had around the farm before—and, more important, a better mind.

"Black Sand," she repeated, while the colt danced beneath her. "I like it. We have black sand on our beach at home. Let me take him outside," she added eagerly. "He's so full of run; it will do him a lot of good."

Alec opened the gate. She was right, and she might as well start working at once. Although she didn't know it, she already had the job.

"You'll find a well-traveled path beyond the barns," he said. "Keep to it. It'll take you along the edge of the fields." He was no longer concerned about her safety. One could not ride as she did without knowing her mount. Black Sand was impatient but standing still. He did not feel the weight of her body so much as he did the weight of her knowledge and understanding.

Pam took Black Sand through the gate at a slow walk, restraint evident in his every stride.

Alec said, "You'll go through a bit of woods. It'll be a good change of scenery for him, but watch out there." He knew that she was as eager as the colt to be off again. She leaned over the colt's withers and whispered into

22

his ear, "Go!" Black Sand leaped forward in a furious bound, and she was ready for it.

Alec watched them go, then headed for his jeep. By driving to the far end of the field, he would be able to see the greater part of her ride. Not that he believed he'd change his mind about hiring her; it was more to confirm what he already knew.

3 ◆ *Joy to the World!*

The girl and her horse sped across the meadow. A red cardinal flew from the heart of a thicket, frightened by their charge. Its clear, loud whistle rose above the sound of the colt's hoofs. From somewhere above, too, came the caws of crows and the scream of a broad-winged hawk, all of them angry with this girl and her horse for disrupting the peace and stillness of the meadow.

Nearing the wooded ridge, Pam slowed the colt to almost a walk and followed a hoof-trampled path into the woods. She stroked Black Sand's lathered neck, and at her touch he sought to bound forward again. She laughed silently and gave in to him, letting him lengthen his strides through the woods. The way was clear and the footing good; there was no need to walk when his heart was so full of run.

A wild carpet of moss glided beneath the colt's flying feet. Squirrels, terrified by the thunder coming down on them, scurried to trees and climbed speedily for self-protection. A rabbit flattened himself out in a hollow. Black Sand raced through open areas, too, masses of wild flowers, dandelions and buttercups, a thousand colored heads, all dancing in the spring breeze.

The path grew narrow with trees and brush closing in upon them. Pam slowed Black Sand to a canter, careful that there were no obstacles in his path. Long, willowy branches slapped against her body.

Suddenly, the colt reared, uttered an insane neighing shriek and, in a single leap, charged off the path. She managed to keep her seat, realizing what had happened. The tree branches had lashed him and he had taken them for a whip.

The trees closed in on her as Black Sand crashed through the brush, fighting her hands at every stride. Repeatedly, branches lashed him until, finally, he reached the open field. He came to an abrupt halt and rose twisting in the air, then plunged. She lost her stirrups and was flung headlong through the air. She landed on the ground, tucking her legs beneath her, her knees to her stomach and her head protected under her arms. She rolled like a human ball, over and over.

When Pam opened her eyes, she saw Black Sand a short distance away. She moved her head slowly and carefully from one side to the other, then one by one, she tried her arms and legs. She was bruised but unbroken. Lying very still, she waited, her eyes on the colt. "You did not trick me," she called to him. "It was my mistake not to be more careful."

Her face was pressed against the hard earth beneath the thickness of the grass. The morning had become strangely quiet, not a cry from bird or animal—nothing. A faint breeze floated over the meadow, bathing her wet brow with a coolness. She flattened her body still more in the grass, enjoying the fresh smell of it, and began humming while keeping her eyes on the colt.

Black Sand, no more than a dozen strides away, heard her. There was no wildness or terror left in his eyes. She continued humming, softly, but the sound carried to his ears.

Finally, Pam raised the upper part of her body stiffly and called to him. Her voice was as soft, as tender, as her humming. She waited several minutes. The colt returned to his grazing, then stopped to look at her again.

Now his movements were in her direction rather than away. She let her head fall back to the grass and continued humming, content to wait, knowing he could not be hurried. He would come to her in his own good time or not at all.

Although her eyes were closed, she could hear the

sound of his hoofs as he approached her. Finally, the hoofbeats stilled and she felt his warm breath on her skin. She opened her eyes and looked up at him, then reached for the dangling stirrup iron. Pulling herself to her feet, she wrapped her arms around his neck and flattened her cheek against him.

Alec drove his jeep back to the barns and awaited Pam's return. He had witnessed her fall and had been ready to go to her when she'd raised her body and apparently called to Black Sand. Knowing that she was all right and that the moment was critical between her and the colt, he had stayed out of it.

What would she tell him, he wondered. Anything at all? If, to protect her job, she said nothing of her fall, then how could he trust her with the responsibilities of the farm? She was bound to make other mistakes, as did every horseman; the danger was in concealment.

She rode up to him in an easy canter, the smell of sweat and weariness upon her and the foam-wet colt. She smiled at him despite it and said, "He unloaded me but he didn't run off." Her voice was gay and friendly but curious, too, wondering how he'd take it.

"I didn't watch out as you said to do," she added. "The tree branches lashed him and he tossed me. But he didn't leave," she repeated.

"Yes, that's a step forward," Alec agreed.

"Please hold him a second," she said, dismounting.

He watched her run quickly to her old car and return

with a carrot. She bit the end off and spit it back into her hand, extending it to Black Sand. When the colt took it from her, she said, "Now we're friends. We've broken bread together." She touched her lips to his muzzle.

Alec knew he'd have great trouble with Henry by hiring Pam. Moreover, he realized that he probably wouldn't be able to keep her there, regardless of how well she did the job. She had said she did not want to be committed for a long period of time. That alarm clock she carried in her head would go off, telling her it was time to move on.

Pam was looking at him intently and he wondered how much she'd read in his eyes. "You've got the job, if you still want it," he said.

"Oh, I do," she answered thoughtfully. Then she turned away and said, "I'll wash him down now. He needs it."

Alec's gaze followed her as she led Black Sand to the barn. It seemed incredible, but she looked braver, prouder, freer than anyone he knew—yet she was only a young girl. Henry would try to attach every reason but the right one to his hiring her.

The confrontation would come soon, for Alec was due back at Aqueduct race track in New York City the following day. The Black was going to race the latter part of the week. Alec decided it would be best to put off mentioning Pam until after the race. If the Black won, as expected, Henry would be in good spirits and might possibly accept a girl working for them.

4 ◆ Post Time

At Aqueduct, the following Saturday, the Black was saddled for the feature race on the afternoon program. Stripped of all useless fat and flesh, he was in his finest shape.

He seemed to know he had never looked so handsome, for he feigned impatience and rebellion against Alec, who stood at his head. The Black pawed the ground and half-reared; his mane, so carefully brushed and combed only moments before, fell tousled about his head and neck. The pure curve of his high, crested neck arched majestically and his great eyes flashed fire as he surveyed the other horses in the saddling paddock.

"Hold him still, won't you?" Henry Dailey said, tightening the girth strap; his voice was gruff, as if speaking to an employee instead of to Alec. Henry's forehead was so deeply wrinkled that his eyebrows were separated from his gray hair only by a thin line of skin.

When the old man had the girth as he wanted it, he straightened and placed a hand on the lead pad beneath the saddle.

"No horse should carry so much weight, but we'll show 'em. We're dodging nobody."

Alec said not a word, knowing nothing was expected of him. Henry was talking for his own benefit. The heavy weights that track handicappers were assigning to the Black in every race he entered must eventually set a turf record. They created a lot of tension before a race so Alec understood and tolerated his old friend's gruffness.

The weights were assigned in order to give every horse in a race a chance at first money. The impost each horse carried on his back was made by taking into consideration his race records, his workouts and his physical condition. Lead weights inserted in a pad beneath the saddle were added, when necessary, to the weight of the rider in order to meet the track handicapper's assigned impost. Champions carried the highest weights of all, and the Black was consistently carrying more weight than any other horse in racing.

Henry stepped back, a stocky man with a barrel-shaped chest. His eyes, like his mouth, were narrow slits

in a round-cheeked face. His nose was his only prominent feature, being hooked, almost like the beak of a
bird of prey. He examined the stallion's hocks and forelegs, the solidity of his flanks and chest, looking for any
sign of soreness or weakness.

The paddock judge called, "Riders, mount your
horses, please!"

Alec was boosted into the saddle and, picking up the
reins, he spoke quietly to the Black. Once Alec was up,
the stallion usually settled down, his nervousness being
quickly replaced by an eagerness to get on with the business of racing. The Black didn't like to wait.

"Any instructions?" Alec asked Henry. The trainer
had mounted Napoleon, their stable pony, and was ac-
companying them to the post.

Henry shook his head. "Just ride your race," he said,
grabbing the Black's bridle. "There's nothing I can tell
you that you don't already know." He moved Napoleon's hindquarters between the Black and a horse following too closely behind.

The red-coated bugler, wearing shiny black boots and
a black hunting cap, stood in the middle of the track, a
long coach horn pressed to his lips. Henry shivered with
anticipation at the sound of the call to the post. He had
lost count of how many years ago it was that he had
heard it for the first time. He was as old and gray and
sway-backed as the gelding he rode, and just as fat.
But each of them still had a job to do.

The great stands were packed and overflowing. Every-

31

body was tense. Everybody was waiting. There were nine horses in the post parade for the Roseben Handicap, a distance of seven furlongs (seven-eighths of a mile) for a purse of $25,000. But the crowd saw only one entry, the Black.

Everybody knew the champion would not be found wanting in speed, but there was always racing luck to consider . . . plus the heavy impost of 138 pounds on his back against light-weighted horses, some carrying only 103 pounds. Besides, it was a short race for the Black. He might have trouble catching the others before the finish if his rider made a single mistake. There would be bumping and swerving in so large a field. So this might be a day to remember, the day the greatest handicap runner of all time was beaten, and they would have been there to see it!

Alec wrapped the reins about his hands and found himself suddenly thinking of Pam again. Had he been wrong in not telling Henry right away that he'd hired a girl? But the trainer hadn't asked how things were going at the farm. He had been too involved in getting ready for this race. Now almost a week had gone by, and Alec wondered how Pam was doing with Black Sand and the others.

At the starting gate, Henry left him. Between the Black's ears Alec could see the sun dropping behind the New York City skyscrapers to the west. He glanced at the other horses and had no fear of them. It was only their riders who could beat him. They were among the best in the business and capable of taking quick advantage of any mistake he might make, even helping him to make a big one that would cost the Black a victory.

They were on either side of him, milling behind the gate, awaiting assistant starters to lead their mounts into the padded, narrow stalls. Each rode slowly, whip in hand and ready. Their faces disclosed no emotion of any kind. They all might have been carved out of wood or cut from toughest leather. Their bodies were hard and fit beneath glossy silks; lips were thin and tightly clasped, looking cruel, as did their narrowed eyes.

Alec was one of them, and had been for a long time. He thought of Pam and the pure joy in her face when she'd ridden Black Sand. Was it to recall such things again, things long forgotten, that he wanted her around?

"Get down to business," he cautioned himself.

A moment later he rode the Black into the Number 1 stall. The other riders followed him into the gate, their voices rising above the din, hard and arrogant, shouting at each other and to the starter. All of them had supreme confidence in their ability to wring every last ounce of speed out of their mounts by the use of massive wrists and broad, thick hands. Slim, all muscle and bone, they sat their racing machines and waited.

Alec pulled down his goggles, his eyes on the lonely, empty battlefield before him. He was ready to go, legs raised at a sharp angle of knee to thigh, back slanted, shoulders hunched, muscles tense. He pressed his face against the Black.

"The most splendid gift of all is a noble horse," he recalled Pam saying. But he shouldn't be thinking of her now.

The bell clanged and the stall doors flew open! Instinctively, Alec let the reins slide through his hands, his voice joining the cries of the other riders, "Yah! Yah! Yah!"

His hands suddenly tightened on the reins again, squeezing rather than pulling, as a horse moved directly in front of them and stayed there. Alec looked for racing room, knowing he'd been caught unprepared. He was furious with himself for having allowed his mind to turn to Pam, to anything but the race. He tried every trick he knew to get the Black free of the rush of bodies on every side of him.

His whip came hissing down, not touching the Black, in an attempt to scare off the packed horses and riders. The wind carried his shouts to the other jockeys, his words threatening and challenging, those of a rider fighting for racing room and, perhaps, his very life. He drove his heels into the Black's sides and his hands went forward in brutal suddenness, urging the horse forward with all his strength.

They raced down the long backstretch chute. There were three furlongs to go to the far turn, two furlongs around the bend, and two more furlongs for home. He had to get the Black free and running before they reached the turn, for the stallion's long strides made it difficult to negotiate turns and he was apt to run out,

34

losing ground. There might not be enough distance left in the stretch run to overtake the leaders.

Alec looked for a clear way through the traffic jam. He let the Black out another notch, not truly knowing where he was going but going anyway, for his need to do *something* was very great. He felt not only anger with himself but guilt. He sought relief in speed and more speed, and danger as well.

He had made a mistake, but there was time to correct it. He leaned into the Black, taking him over to the rail, only to pull him up abruptly when the opening he had spotted was closed by a plunging horse. Alec took the stallion back, moving him toward the middle of the pack, only inches away from the heaving hindquarters of horses directly ahead.

The Black was fighting for his head, trying to run over the horses in front of him. Beyond the bunched field, two horses were free and clear. Light-weighted sprinters, their legs moved in short, piston-like strides, taking them toward the far turn like small, wound-up whirlwinds. Alec knew he had to get after them soon or the Black would be beaten.

He tried to move the stallion between two outside horses but was shut off again. He had to bring the Black almost to a stop to avoid going down; his hands took a tight hold on the reins and he jerked hard. The force of it wrenched the bit in the stallion's mouth, tearing the flesh at the corners.

He heard the Black scream in rage and pain, and his

35

heart felt a deep anguish. Yet he'd had no alternative if he wanted to avoid serious injury—even death. Suddenly he saw an opening and launched the Black forward again.

Lathered foam whipped from the stallion's neck as he shot between horses. None of the jockeys had expected such a rush from behind with so little room between them. Above the din of racing hoofs, Alec heard the challenges the other riders hurled at him. One false step and the Black would go down. He guided him through the mass of horseflesh in a single rush, avoiding hoofs and bodies by inches. He rode as he never had before, using all his wits and skill with a strength and harshness he had not known he possessed. His daring, combined with the Black's fury and speed astonished the others and threw them off balance. They separated, and the leaping black stallion sped between them, free and clear!

Leaving the pack behind, Alec took the Black into the turn with only the two front-running sprinters ahead. They were setting a dizzy pace. Had he still the time and distance to catch them? The Black devoured the track with his long strides, yet ran wide going around the turn. Alec tried to guide him over to the rail but his extreme speed made it impossible. The leaders were already leaving the turn and entering the homestretch with just two furlongs to go.

Alec flattened himself against the stallion's neck, his face buried in the mane. There was no need to urge the

Black on, for the racing stallion knew what was expected of him. He came off the turn, stretched low to the ground in the fury of his run. He was catching the leaders fast, outrunning them with every magnificent stride.

The crowd was on its feet. Was this to be the day the Black lost for the first time? The two leaders flashed by the sixteenth pole, their strides coming as one, a closely matched team of two, fighting, clawing their way to the finish wire.

The Black came down the track with a swiftness that could not be denied. But the fans were not really aware of the awesome power of his body, for he ran with such ease that his strides seemed to be a single flowing movement.

The finish wire was far enough away for Alec to know that the distance had not run out on them. He shouted into the wind created by his horse. Only the Black heard his cry of victory, but he was the only one that mattered. He caught the leaders two strides from the wire and swept under it all by himself.

5 ◆ Sexism

Back in the stable area, Henry asked Alec, "You were caught napping at the start. Why?"

Alec shrugged his shoulders. "We made up for it," he said.

Henry didn't persist. It was not uncommon for a rider to make a mistake in the break from the gate—or even to know the fear of death. Many rode recklessly immediately afterward, as Alec had done, as if by daring fate to strike them down, they were able to regain their nerve and courage.

Henry decided to change the subject. His gaze followed a hot-walker going by, cooling out a chestnut horse that had been in the last race of the afternoon.

"What kind of a boy is that?" he asked sarcastically.

Despite the soiled blue jeans, sweatshirt and peaked cap, the walker had the unmistakable configuration of a female.

"The right size but the wrong sex," Henry continued. The girl was about five feet one inch tall and weighed around 100 pounds, the ideal size for a rider. "Too bad. She'd like to have been a boy."

"I don't think she wants to be anything but what she is," Alec said. He had seen this girl one evening in the lobby of a local movie, wearing high heels and a short skirt. Her hair had been as slick and polished as any mane she'd ever tended. What had been slim, hard boyishness during the day was girlish slenderness and softness at night. And the young jockey with her, whom he'd recognized too, had not taken his eyes from her for a moment, holding her arm and opening doors. Yet, all day long, she had carried her own pails, mucked stalls, cleaned horses and laundry and tack.

"I don't like to see girls around horsemen," Henry said. "Just because of their sex they create problems we wouldn't have otherwise. It takes a man's mind off his work. They get emotionally involved with horses, everything."

"Is it any different from other businesses?"

"Sure. Ours is rough; it's not for girls," Henry said emphatically. "I think a woman should be a woman and

39

a mother and everything that goes with it."

Alec had heard all this before. Henry spoke of a woman's *femininity* as though he had respect for it, but he didn't. Alec had seen the old trainer with many girls in the stable area, and his attitude was always so severe and authoritative that he awed them to the point of fear. Perhaps it was his way of showing them they didn't belong there. He reproached them for what he considered to be wavering courage in handling their horses or feminine weakness in doing their jobs. His experienced eyes never failed to perceive their fright, weariness, carelessness—and he despised them for it. They, in turn, despised him.

Alec thought of Pam, and decided it was no time to bring up the fact that he had hired her, providing Henry didn't talk about the farm. Yet in her defense, as well as the defense of all girls working at the track, he said, "You've got to admit that they keep tack and stalls cleaner than most men, and they seem to have more patience with the horses. They coax them rather than use a hard hand."

Henry laughed. "They're good at coaxing *anything,* that's for sure, men as well as horses. Otherwise, trainers wouldn't hire 'em."

Alec said nothing. All his life he had been taught to have respect for older people, to accept the fact that their age and experience gave them the privilege to set the rules. Not that they were always right, he knew, or even that they claimed to be. But there should be no open questioning of their authority, and certainly no defiance.

He knew that most trainers felt more or less like Henry when it came to hiring women, but there was a labor shortage at the track. Not too many men wanted the job of caring for a race horse, day and night, seven days a week. They could find other work that was less confining.

Alec looked around the area at the stablehands working in the late afternoon sun, enjoying its warmth and softness, laughing and talking while they scrubbed leg bandages in iron tubs, hung their laundry, cleaned tack, bedded stalls and fed horses, all to blaring radios. Some wouldn't be done until long after dark and their day had begun well before 6:00 A.M.

All that most people knew about horse racing was the front side of the track, Alec decided, the big names of horses and trainers and jockeys—perhaps thirty-five in number. Fans knew little, if anything, about the backside.

The grooms knew their horses better than anybody, yet they waited like children to get what the front side gave them, which wasn't much. New York City tracks were better than most, and yet the take-home pay for grooms was only about $90 a week, if they were lucky. Out of that had to come food and clothing and rent for themselves and their families. They had no union, no pension fund, no hospitalization, no way of improving their conditions, and certainly no job security. They could be fired on a moment's notice.

Worse still, there was little unity among them. Discord prevailed. There were tensions and resentment between groups—racial among black, white and Puerto Rican; old men against young men; family men against single men; and, finally, men against women.

Why then did they work here? Alec had heard their reasons. They liked horses. The work was not hard even if continuous. They had to work somewhere. If they'd had sufficient schooling they wouldn't be here. And for those who were young and had the ability, there was the opportunity of becoming exercise boys and galloping horses for $110 a week, with dreams of becoming jockeys.

Henry said, "Like I've told you before, Alec, I've nothing against girls but . . ."

Always the *but*, Alec thought, and now would come the ugly words, usually with some justification but based on the clear-cut classifications Henry had worked out years ago. In those days males and females had been forced to fit the typical pattern of stereotyping—the man being masculine and strong, the woman feminine and weak, if not altogether helpless.

"This is just another *movement* of women trying to compete with men," Henry continued. "And in this business it's dynamite!"

In Alec's opinion there was nothing explosive about women trying to get an even break. As with all minority groups, they were trying to get a piece of the action, equality of opportunity. He kept his silence, knowing that his beliefs—if he expressed them—would do no good. Henry's tirade against women was based on emotion, not logic.

Yet Alec had to say something, for Henry was looking at him, waiting for him to agree. He took another line. "You've seen plenty of girls who can do more with a horse than a man."

"Then they should stick to horse shows and rodeos," Henry said bitterly, "where they're treated like women. They're dynamite here, like I said. There's too much tension already in racing. If they push for a bigger role in it, they'll face conflicts that exist in no other business. There are too many around now, and soon they'll be dealing from a position of strength. That's when it will explode; men won't let women take their jobs!"

Alec turned back to the crowded stable area. Was the battle of the sexes different here from any place else? Women at the track expected ridicule and ugly words. Some were plain uncomfortable, yet lived with it. Others were frightened by threats of being roughed up or, in the case of those who worked horses, being ridden into the rail. Yes, Alec admitted to himself, there were great differences here, depending upon the job. Women were the equal of men in everything but brute strength, which sometimes became very necessary at the track.

Yet these women were so needed, so necessary and qualified for the work. They should not be eliminated as Henry and others would like to see done. There was no such thing as "men only" jobs when it came to the love and care and skill required in the handling of horses. What right had men to think so? Sex prejudice was no less evil than racial or religious bias, Alec decided.

His gaze returned to Henry. Did he need to agree with him simply because the old man expected him to do so?

"We've hired a girl ourselves," Alec heard himself say quietly.

"What?"

"I said, we've hired a girl. She's at the farm, working the colts. I had to fire the new man; he was drunk."

Henry did not reply immediately, and the silence was heavy with tension. Finally, he asked, "But you hired a *girl* in his place? Why?" It was clear he just couldn't understand. He really wanted to know. "I've explained to you a hundred times . . ."

"I know," Alec said, "a hundred times I've heard it."

"And still you hired her?"

"She's good, and she's at the farm, not here."

"She'll be here," Henry said. "It's what they all want, every single one of 'em. She's using you as a back door, but she'll be here."

"Not her. Besides she wants the job for only a short while. She said she'll be moving on soon," he added persuasively.

"She'll be moving on, heh," Henry said. "One of those rootless kids. I know her kind all right, and they're the worst. Spoiled daughters of upper- and middle-class America, full of romantic self-pity and vanity."

"How can you say that, when you haven't met her?"

"I told you I know her *kind*. I've seen hundreds. A good spanking at an early age would have saved everyone the trouble of putting up with her nonsense and kept her home where she belonged. Well, she's not goin' to solve her emotional problems at our place. Why'd you ever let her get to you, Alec?"

"It was no earth-shattering decision I had to make in hiring her. She's competent. She can do the job."

"And pretty?" Henry asked. "I suppose she's pretty."

"Yes, she's that too," Alec answered, knowing Henry regarded a girl's beauty as the essence of her feminine worth.

Henry chuckled. "So that's the reason you hired her. Now, I see." He put an arm around Alec's shoulders, as if to show his understanding of Alec's male response to an attractive girl. "But you should keep all that separate from business," he went on, man to man. "Handling those colts is a responsible job, if they're to be brought to racing form. An inexperienced rider can wreck their wind and incentive to race. You know it as well as I do, Alec. You'd better just tell that girl to move on now. Tell her tonight. I'll watch over things here. Nothing much to do for a few days, anyway. Do what you have to do an' enjoy yourself." Still smiling, he winked at Alec, one male to another.

Alec said quietly, "You've never seen her ride, yet

you don't want her around."

"I don't want her around *our* place," Henry said. "Where she goes is not my business, but running Hopeful Farm is."

His voice was the voice of authority and obviously he expected Alec to be aware of it. At Hopeful Farm he ruled over the exercise, training and education of the horses. He determined the age at which they should face their first competition. He trained them, had their faults corrected, and brought their speed to highest pitch. He treated their wounds and sprains. He knew their virtues and their weaknesses. And, finally, he taught Alec to ride each of them so that the union between horse and rider was as near perfect as possible.

"You mean," Alec persisted, "she must be turned down flat for no reason other than——"

"She's a girl and therefore not acceptable to me," Henry interrupted. "Tell her that. She'll understand without your going into it. You won't have any trouble."

"Not acceptable," Alec repeated. "Do you realize what would happen if you said that to a black man? You'd have the explosion here you've always talked about."

"That's exactly what I want to avoid by not having her around," Henry said.

"You're not avoiding it," Alec said. "You're *asking* for it." He'd never spoken to Henry so harshly before.

The man's lined face tightened, his eyes furious. Yet he controlled his anger, saying gently, "We're not talking about racism, Alec."

46

"*Sexism* is as bad," Alec said. "I can't fire her because she's a girl."

"Then you'll have to decide between her and me," Henry said, his voice still under control but not his eyes.

"You're kidding," Alec said.

"Try me and see."

"But that's ridiculous. You mean because of a girl you'd go? I don't believe you, Henry."

"You'd better believe me, Alec. It's your choice. Go to the farm and make up your mind." Henry turned and walked away, leaving Alec alone.

6 • *Wild Flowers and the Blues*

It was late, the night cool and very dark, when Alec arrived at Hopeful Farm. He drove directly to the training barn, wanting to see Pam and have the whole thing over as quickly as possible. Then he'd be able to sleep.

He had decided he must let her go. It wouldn't be fair to have her stay in the face of Henry's open opposition and hostility. She'd be blamed outrageously for anything that went wrong whether or not it was her fault, and much could happen in the handling of two-year-olds.

When Alec had left Aqueduct, he'd been determined

to fight Henry's prejudice by keeping Pam and finding out what the old man would do about it. He really didn't think Henry would walk out on them, after all their years together, because of a girl. It was all too ridiculous and childish. But how could he be certain?

"Try me and see," the trainer had said, sounding as if he meant it.

Alec had never defied Henry and yet, he told himself, there was a principle involved here that went deeper than his desire to keep a competent person on the payroll. Now that he had made his decision to let Pam go, he wondered if he was not losing more than Pam's services by giving in to Henry.

Leaving the car, Alec paused in his tracks, waiting for his eyes to become accustomed to the darkness. There was no wind and Alec breathed deeply the smells of the country. He sniffed the scent of new grass and the warm bodies of horses, different here from the race track. The mares had been turned out with their suckling foals and he could see their dark figures in the field. No sounds reached his ears. The darkness and the silence were familiar to him.

His gaze followed the miles of white fence. There were hundreds of acres of the finest land that could be bought, dozens of fenced paddocks and sheds and barns, all used for the specific purpose of raising race horses. It was a costly business but no other could compare with it as far as he was concerned. He wouldn't want to do anything else or live any place else

Hopeful Farm needed Henry's *fullest* cooperation if it was to win races and breed the best horses. No one could take his place in skill and experience. Alec could not risk it all for the sake of keeping a girl on the place, much as he would like to.

Pam would understand when he explained everything to her. With her ability, she would have no trouble finding work elsewhere. He must not feel that he was letting her down—or himself.

Alec walked to the training barn and saw her car parked beside it. The flowers painted on the car would infuriate Henry if he saw them. But he wouldn't. He wouldn't even be here . . . yet Pam still had to go.

Entering the barn, Alec walked down the long corridor of box stalls, all occupied by the two-year-olds in training. He stopped before one and, peering through the bars at Black Sand, called softly, "Hello, fellow. Come on over."

The colt shook himself and remained where he was. He lowered his long neck to the water bucket, playing rather than drinking, blowing into the water and splattering the spray about the stall and Alec.

Alec stepped back. "Okay," he said. "See you in the morning then."

He had already heard the faint sound of music coming from the apartment above. He glanced at the ceiling, then with fast strides he headed for the stairs. He'd made his decision, and there was no sense putting off what he had to do. He bounded up the steps, taking two at a time, as if by hurrying he would give himself no time to change his mind.

The door was already ajar when he knocked on it, pushing it even farther open. "Pam," he called. "I'd like to see you."

There was no answer, only the music, softly played— a blues beat that he knew was popular with young people but not very familiar to him. One had to take time and effort to understand today's music, and he had neither.

"Pam!" he called louder and more impatiently. He pushed the door half-open, but remained where he was, not wanting to intrude upon her privacy.

The lights were on and, looking inside, he found the change in the apartment hard to believe. The furniture had been moved around and the chairs and couch were covered with a bright, new fabric. There were cut flowers everywhere, wild ones from the fields, lilacs and pink-and-white dogwood, buttercups and dandelions, all filling vases and glasses and even paper cups. On the walls were posters of every description—psychedelic art of colorful, intricate design; surfers within the curl of gigantic waves; rock groups, jazz groups, blues groups and music festivals.

Alec felt his insides tighten as he thought what would have happened had Henry seen them. "Pam!" he shouted. "Are you here? It's Alec."

The music ended, and the portable phonograph automatically turned itself off. He stepped inside. The apartment was a combination living room–bedroom arrangement with a kitchen at the end, concealed by a large screen. Pam had hung a large fish net, complete with cork floats over the screen, and on it were placed sea shells of every description and shroud-like veils of Spanish moss. He wondered at her carrying so much with her wherever she went—the shells and the posters and everything else in the room.

Alec went to the soft-cushioned chair beside the phonograph. She'd been reading, for there was a paperback book on the end table and a half-finished glass of milk. He glanced at the book title, *Selected Poems (1956-1968)* by Leonard Cohen. There were other books in a neat pile beside the chair. He didn't know what made him sit down and take them, one by one, to look at each —unless it was to know her better in the short time he had left.

The Complete Works of Lewis Carroll. He was surprised he knew only two of the stories, *Alice's Adventures in Wonderland* and *Through the Looking Glass,* when there were so many others and poems as well. He picked up the other books, Joseph Conrad's *Heart of Darkness; The Stranger* by Albert Camus; *King Solomon's Ring* by Konrad Lorenz; Bullfinch's *Mythology;* and a couple of books featuring the adventures of *Dr. Dolittle,* which he'd thought were read only by little kids.

Alec got to his feet, wondering if he should leave and talk to her in the morning. It was very late. Obviously, she was around somewhere; perhaps walking in the fields as she would likely do. Being in this apartment, which she had made her own in so short a period of time, made it all the more difficult for him to tell her she had to go. Tomorrow, he decided, it would be easier for him and for her.

He left a note, telling her he would see her in the morning, and was about to leave when he saw her stack of record albums. Buddy Guy. He had never heard of him. There were names of other musicians as unfamiliar. John Mayall, Larry Coryell, Bob Dylan, Eric Clapton, Joan Baez, Tim Buckley—who were they?

Pam lived in a world very different from his own, he decided. But she wasn't rootless, as Henry had claimed. She took her home with her wherever she traveled, including her family.

On the coffee table was an open picture album of pocket size. He picked it up and looked at the faces. Obviously they were her family, all of them on a Florida beach in bathing suits, as tanned as she—two young brothers, a younger sister with hair golden in the sun like Pam's, her mother and father, all smiling and looking very happy and content with their lives. There were pictures too of a black Great Dane, a small Australian Terrier, two Siamese cats and her Arabian mare, Tena, a glowing chestnut with a broad white blaze running down to a narrow snip at the nostrils. These people and pets all looked far too pleasant to have been left behind. He wondered that she had gone and that her parents had let her.

"*I know her kind,*" Henry had said. "*Spoiled daugh-*

*ters . . . I've seen hundreds . . . A good spanking at
an early age would have kept her home."*

Was it another case of Henry stereotyping someone
he could not understand? His need to speak in generali-
ties, in great bursts of ignorance and rage?

Alec did not think it had been easy for Pam to leave
home—or for her parents to say good-by. There was
much more he would like to know about her.

Alec left the apartment, not looking forward to what
he had to do the next morning.

7 • *Black Pepper*

Alec found it no easier to tell Pam in the morning; if anything, it was worse. He had slept very little, and then only after daybreak, so he arrived at the barn after Pam had begun work and was on the track. He had wanted to see her before she became involved in anything, so she could pack and leave without postponing her departure another day.

The two stablemen assigned to the barn were cleaning stalls, but the horses were in Pam's care. The men's eyes followed him, knowing the importance of his inspection as he went from stall to stall, examining each horse, one by one.

It took Alec longer than usual, and he wondered if he was unconsciously looking for something with which to find fault, making it easier for him to let her go. But the horses' eyes and coats shone with good health from proper attention.

He shouldn't have expected anything else, he decided. She was the kind of person who took care of horses to make them happy, not to impress anyone else. The only reward she asked was that her charges be stronger and healthier from her pleasure in the task.

Alec went to the large daybook chart on the wall of the tack room. On it were the names of the ten two-year-olds in training, and beneath each was a daily work schedule which he had given her before leaving for Aqueduct. He had asked her to keep to it as closely as possible, and to make any notes she wanted about the progress of each horse.

She had already ridden three horses that morning and her penciled comments were there. Black Sand had gone a half-mile easily in 50 seconds, breaking from the starting gate. She noted that he was ready for faster works.

Alec was inclined to agree with her. Black Sand was the toughest colt they had in the barn and the most precocious. If she could get him in hand, he would be ready to race this season. He was more apt to win at shorter distances than the longer ones that came later

56

in the year. There were other horses that Alec preferred for distance races, such as the two she'd galloped after Black Sand—one for two miles, the other for three. The last one needed his shoes re-set, Pam had noted on the chart.

She was now riding Black Pepper, the only filly in the barn. A good one, Alec thought, but with a pea-sized brain. Black Pepper had everything else a race horse needed; he had high hopes for her despite her lack of sense. Pam was to break the filly from the gate and go a half-mile in a slow 55 or 56 seconds. He was taking it easy with the filly, for she had the breeding necessary to go the longer, more important races next year. Her problem was understanding what she was supposed to do; handling her in the starting gate had not been easy.

Grabbing a saddle and bridle, Alec left the tack room. "Sam," he called to one of the men, "when did Pam leave with the last one?"

"Just before you got here. She won't have reached the track yet."

A few minutes later, Alec led a rangy bay colt out of the barn. With a hand on the horse's withers, he vaulted into the saddle without touching the stirrups. And with it, in a single second, he turned into another person, forgetting momentarily the real purpose of his visit. Every part of him fell into balance as he rode off at a canter.

Black Pepper's education at the gate had begun as a yearling, he reflected, along with all the others. But unlike the rest, she'd given them nothing but trouble. Each time she continued to act as if it was the first time. Either she was just plain dumb, as he suspected, or she was as obstinate and cantankerous as her dam, Black Minx.

However, Black Minx had won the Kentucky Derby, so her filly was worth all the time and trouble it might take to bring her along slowly until she broke from the gate properly. Being a filly she could not stand as much abuse as a colt, so Pam's patience and light hands might be exactly what was needed.

Alec saw them in the distance and closed his legs about the colt, sending him into a faster gallop. Black Out, the colt he was riding, was rugged and ungainly. He'd been slow in coming along, and Henry had wisely decided to reserve him until next year. But Black Out was intelligent and did everything right, including breaking from the gate. Perhaps he could teach the filly what it was all about. At least it would help Pam to have another horse in the gate. Horses should always be broken from the gate in pairs at least, never singly; and preferably there should be three or four. But that was one of the things they had been unable to do that year.

Alec caught up to Pam just as she reached the training track. She glanced back and said, "I expected you a long time ago. You missed Black Sand, the best part."

"I'll see him tomorrow."

"Good," she said. "I'm glad you're staying."

Her voice had the gay, friendly, singing quality he re-

58

membered. He looked at her, suddenly aware of what he'd said about *tomorrow,* as if he'd had no intention of telling her that she must leave today.

She wore no ponytail that morning, he noticed. Her long, thick, wild blond hair waved and floated below her shoulders. Her clothes were jeans, a white blouse and brown, worn loafers. No boots; no masculinity. And in the filly's mane were braided flowers of yellow, pink and blue.

She swung her shoulders and turned Black Pepper around. "Come on," she said. "Let's go! It's a beautiful day." Her wonderful gaiety blossomed under the morning sun, and Alec was glad he had decided to ride with her.

They came to a stop behind the four-horse starting gate. Max, the man who operated it, was there waiting for them.

"Have you had any trouble with her?" Alec asked, nodding to the filly.

"Lots," she said, "but she'll come around. It takes time." She ran her hand down the filly's right foreleg as far as she could reach. "She's a little sore here," Pam said.

"The trouble's not down there," Alec said, "but in her head."

Surprisingly, because he knew she loved all horses despite their faults, she agreed emphatically with him. "I sure know that," Pam said. "She has a mental block of some kind. Maybe it's something like claustrophobia in a person. She can't take that narrow stall with the doors closed."

"Let's try it," Alec said. "If she can't stand still, she'll never start."

He watched Pam ride toward the gate, her hand stroking the filly with astonishing delicacy, trying to reassure Black Pepper that there was nothing to fear from the contraption ahead. The filly whinnied with high spirits but Alec wondered how long it would last. Perhaps forever with such a girl in the saddle—if he could only have given her time.

His big-boned colt moved forward in powerful but ungainly strides, so different from those of the slender filly ahead of him. Black Pepper moved with deerlike grace, her eyes very feminine, gentle and timid. Yet she would be rough to handle, Alec decided, if she went into one of her uncalled-for tantrums. Somehow, they must channel all that fire burning inside her—the hustling, bustling blood of her dam—into competing against other horses. She shouldn't expend all her energy in the starting gate.

Walking up to Black Pepper, Max took hold of the filly's bridle and sought to lead her into the gate. She swung around in a tight circle, dragging him with her.

Pam didn't seem to be disturbed by her mount's antics. She was patting the filly, taking her time and speaking softly. Her figure concealed the small saddle on which she sat, so that it looked as if she and the filly shared the same skin.

Black Pepper suddenly twisted and yanked Max off his feet, whirling him around. Pam needed all her skill to keep from being thrown. The filly reared, twisting in the air, and Max had to let go of the bridle.

In the most primitive of instincts, Pam flung her arms around the filly's neck and clung with her hands to the warm, moist flesh. For a moment she and Black Pepper were a single, astonishing creature, their heads side by side, mane and hair entwined, streaming and winging, black and gold.

Alec moved his colt forward and was at her side when the filly came down. "Wow!" Pam said. "I thought she was going to get rid of me that time." Alec noticed that she hid her face from him as long as possible.

"I probably would have been dumped if I'd been on her," he said reassuringly.

She raised her head, and her face was cold and wet. "I'm glad you're here to help," she said. "Every day it's been like this, and it's doing her schooling no good."

"I'll go with you this time," Alec said, moving his big colt closer to the filly and taking hold of her bridle. His mount might be young and clumsy, but he was quiet enough to handle the duties of a stable pony.

They neared the starting stalls and the filly fought to break free of Alec's hold on her bridle. Both he and Pam sought control as Black Pepper lunged directly at the gate, instead of away from it. They managed to stop her before she reached it and backed her up, only to have her fight for her head and plunge forward again.

61

"Crazy, that's what she is," Alec said when they'd brought her to a stop. "First, she won't go near it and now she wants to tear it down."

"*Afraid* is more like it," Pam answered. "Horses can have a psychosis same as people, and she's got a big one. Let me try it another way."

She began whistling softly to the filly, her notes barely audible and without any shrillness. Then she spoke to Black Pepper, her words as tender and enchanting as her whistling had been.

"The time for fear or play or whatever it is that's bothering you is over," she said. "Wait until I tell you to go. There is no hurry, nothing to be afraid of."

Alec waited in silence, knowing that while the filly did not understand Pam's words, the sound of the girl's voice meant something to Black Pepper. What Pam would achieve by this kind of communication, if anything, was unpredictable. It worked with some horses and not with others, depending upon the depth of feeling and the rider's ability to communicate.

He could do nothing but wait. The filly was now in Pam's charge, to handle as she thought best. His job for the present was to stay out of it, while she tried to achieve what had to be done. If she needed help, he would know, and was there to give it. There must be no accident, nothing that would further complicate the education of Black Pepper. He had known other young horses as difficult to school but none any worse. It would take time and patience, but the rewards would be great if and when Black Pepper raced.

With her voice, her legs and her hands, Pam continued speaking to the filly for a long while, without attempting to move her forward. Black Pepper raised her head, turning it back slightly, as if listening to what Pam had to say. Alec, still holding the filly, felt the hot air coming from her wide-open nostrils.

Pam talked, hummed and whistled, never pausing; all with such a rich harmony of happiness and youth, of friendship and joy that Alec found himself responding to her gaiety.

Finally, Pam moved Black Pepper forward. But the filly came to an abrupt stop directly before the open stall, her fear of it evident in the sweating of her flanks. Again, Pam talked to her and the moments passed.

Alec moved his own mount inside the stall, hoping the filly would follow. He could see her out of the corner of his eyes, moving forward foot by foot. Finally, Pam had Black Pepper inside, but with the front and back doors wide open. At least the filly was in the stall, even if she wouldn't stay there for long.

Alec heard Max close the doors behind them and expected Black Pepper to bolt forward at the clank of the metal frames. Surprisingly, she remained still, if not altogether straight and balanced.

Max was on the track before them, ready to close the front doors. He looked at Alec questioningly.

"Close mine first," Alec said.

The grilled flaps closed in front of his big colt, who

made no attempt to bolt through them. "Good boy," Alec said, patting him. The stall quarters were confining but his mount was neither nervous nor curious. He was simply waiting to be turned free. Here was one to be reckoned with next year, Alec decided.

He looked away from the grilled screen to watch Black Pepper as Max carefully closed her stall door, making no sound except for a slight click, which was drowned out by Pam's constant murmurings to the filly.

"Okay, Max," he called softly. "If she stays still, open right away. Don't wait for her to get straightened out." He didn't want to give the filly a chance to fly to pieces inside. If she could just get away while she was quiet, she might learn there was nothing to fear from the gate.

"Come out slowly with her, Pam," he called. "Don't push her."

Pam didn't pause in her murmurings. Black Pepper banged her hoofs against the sides of the stall, then was quiet. The filly wasn't as straight as she should be, but she could come out without hurting herself. For the time being that was all Alec asked.

"Now, Max," he called. "Open up."

8 ◆ *The Biting Edge*

The starting bell clanged and the doors flew open. Instinctively, without wanting to do it or any need for it, Alec shouted, "Yah! Yah!" as he loosened rein and prodded the big colt forward. Black Out charged from the gate sluggishly but in a straight line.

Alec turned his head quickly to look for the filly. She had left the stall almost at a walk but was now coming on. However, she made for the outside of the track before Pam could get her aimed down the stretch. He saw her slip dangerously but recover.

Alec sat very still, waiting for his big, ungainly colt to

find his balance and settle in stride. He inched up the reins, restraining him in case Black Out had any notion to go faster. All Alec wanted from him was an easy, slow half-mile in 55 or 56 seconds, and the same for the filly.

They flashed by the first furlong pole with three more furlongs to go. Instinctively, Alec began counting off the seconds, down to fifths of seconds, keeping time in his mind. Every jockey needed to know the pace of his mount, whether running at full speed or not. The triple throbbing beat of the colt's hoofs over the track was irregular, but in the months to come he would find his balance and true stride. Alec gave him no more rein than he had from the start, keeping him between a gallop and a run, in what they called a "breeze."

He heard the beat of the filly's hoofs before Black Pepper drew alongside. He felt a sudden competitive urge to give his colt more rein but fought it down. He glanced at Pam and knew that, like him, she was enjoying the taste of the racing wind, their two horses running stride for stride.

The filly pushed out her small head in front of the colt, as if determined to beat him, her sweated neck glittering like black satin in the rays of the sun. Her desire to compete was a good sign. She might even make a great race horse in time, Alec decided—perhaps the equal of her dam, Black Minx.

The seconds ticked away in Alec's mind as the two horses remained locked together, moving as a team around the first sharp turn, both of them inexperienced

66

and running wide. His colt lost a little ground to the filly and he let out a notch in the reins to catch up. They were very evenly matched at this stage of their training.

Racing down the backstretch, Alec called to Pam as they passed the quarter-mile pole, "Thirty and a tick. Let her out a notch."

She nodded her head without turning to him, her blond hair whipping in the wind alongside the black mane. The filly raced a half-length ahead. Alec moved his horse faster, but still kept a little behind, knowing it would give the filly heart and confidence to think she was winning. His own colt was running well within himself and showed no interest in going faster. That would come in time, Alec decided. For now, Black Out was content doing only that which was asked of him.

The filly was something else. For all her antics and stubbornness at the gate, she was running for the sheer love and excitement of it. Pam was having a difficult time holding her back. She was fighting, trying to get her head down and be allowed to run as she pleased.

He saw Pam give in a little, letting her have more rein and drawing a full length in front of the colt. He wondered if she carried a stop watch in her closed hand, and had any idea what she was ticking off in seconds as they passed the third furlong pole with an eighth of a mile to go.

Coming off the final turn, Pam moved the filly still farther ahead, and Alec decided she must be carrying a watch. He, too, moved his mount faster, lengthening

67

strides until he was alongside her. The pace was just right to finish the half-mile in a shade under 55 seconds.

The track was deep and rough going down the home-stretch, making it all the more difficult for Alec's colt to keep his lumbering balance. Alec steadied him, helping him find a path over ground that would not give way beneath his flying hoofs.

They passed the finish pole and, slowing their horses, galloped out another furlong before coming to a stop and turning back.

"Just about right," Alec said. "What'd we do? . . . Fifty-five on the nose?"

She pressed her head against the filly's neck, breathing in the smell of horse, the odor of wet hair and hide. "I think so," she said finally. "It seemed about that to me."

"You mean you don't have a watch?"

"It's in the barn. I forgot it," she said, straightening in her saddle. "I'm sorry. I shouldn't have."

"If you can keep time in your head as good as that, you don't need it," Alec said quietly.

She rode off the track ahead of him, slim, collected and, Alec decided, very proud. She had a right to be, for she'd not only taken the filly from the gate well but had worked in the required time without a watch, and he had been there to see it done. He rode after her, admiring the free and easy way she sat her horse, a horseman whose ride had no goal but the joy of riding. He had never seen a rider and mount more perfectly matched.

For all her natural ability, she'd had professional guidance. He was certain of it.

"How about your father?" he called to her. "Does he ride?"

"He sure does," she answered, without turning her head.

"Is he a professional horseman by any chance?"

"Dad? Oh, no," she said, laughing. "He'd be the first to admit he's no professional. But some of his best friends are," she added. "That's where I've been lucky because they taught me all I know. Captain Bill Heyer was one of them and Stanley White another. Do you know them?"

"No," Alec replied, "but there are many good horsemen I don't know."

Alec continued riding behind her, regretting that he had to tell her she must leave after all she had accomplished. He felt worse as her happiness with the beauty of the morning reached him.

He listened as she exclaimed at the splendor of the great sweep of rolling fields. She pointed out the winged clouds sailing above the wooded ridge in the morning sky. She commented on tree tops and bushes bursting into fiery lights of reds and greens and yellows as the sun reached them and they emerged from morning shadows into bright day. So many things he knew were there but had not really looked at in a long time.

At the barn, they untacked their horses and washed them down, hosing and sponging and swiping them clean. Together they walked them dry before putting them back in their clean box stalls. They talked of horses and the joy of sharing them, but said nothing about the serious business of training and racing. Neither did Alec mention that she must leave by the end of the day.

It was becoming more and more difficult for him. He had allowed her time to become involved in her day's work, and now he was involved in it as well, sharing it with her. Perhaps, he thought, when the work was done it would be easier.

"Five more colts to go," she said, walking through the barn. "Will you ride with me?"

"Why not?" he asked laughing. "I enjoy it as much as you do." He did not say it to please her but because he meant it with all his heart. Standing with her in the midst of the smells, sounds, lights and shadows that filled the barn, he felt more at peace than he had in a long time. It was the completeness of enjoying the horses for the companions they were rather than thinking of them as racing machines whose value depended on how much money they would make for Hopeful Farm. How long had he been thinking of them almost exclusively in those terms, he wondered.

She was looking at him as if she knew what was going on in his mind. He felt guilty and self-conscious. She couldn't have guessed, he thought. She was keen but certainly not clairvoyant.

"Don't you believe me?" he asked finally. "I mean about enjoying myself."

"Oh, I believe you all right," she answered. "You

just look as if you're a little surprised to have said it—almost as if you didn't quite believe it yourself. Perhaps it's been a long time since you've thought of horses as . . ." she turned to the horses and back again ". . . well, *friends.*"

He didn't answer. Suddenly he was angered by her words, her accusation. It was easy for her to say such things, he thought. She had no farm to run, no payroll to meet. She had freedom of movement without any commitments or responsibilities to others.

His face became tense and hard, and he knew this was the opportune time to tell her she had to go, to explain that with Henry feeling the way he did it just wouldn't work out for her to stay.

With Henry feeling the way he did. But why place all the blame on Henry? Alec realized that he had just been using Henry's arguments in justifying his own actions to himself. Was Pam so wrong in what she'd said? Did he have such a need for success, for security, that he had forgotten the most important thing in his life? Was he angered at her or at *himself?*

She had walked over to Black Sand's stall and he followed her, still undecided as to what he should say and hating himself for his indecision. Always before he had been positive in his decisions and he had no use for those who wavered in making up their minds. Was this too part of his training—black was black and white was white, with no shading, no time for doubt or understanding or compassion?

Pam had entered the stall and was braiding a flower in Black Sand's mane. Alec watched but said nothing. It made no difference to him if all the horses in the barn wore flowers, but how would Henry have taken it? There was no point in this girl's ever having a luxurious home when she so obviously preferred a horse barn, he decided. Her whole life was united with manes and shining coats and whinnies. They were only horses and yet without them what would life be like for Pam? Or for that matter for himself.

She turned toward him while taking her hands from Black Sand. He caught the colt's gleaming eyes and said, "Watch out, Pam."

He was too late with his warning. The colt had caught her outstretched hand with his teeth, holding it between his great soft lips. Though it was done as a playful gesture, it could have deadly serious consequences.

Both Pam and Alec remained very quiet. They knew she could not remove her hand from the colt's mouth unless he opened it of his own accord. She dare not make a wrong, hasty move. Any mistake might cause him to sever all her fingers in one chomping bite of his razor-edged teeth.

Alec took a step closer. If he could get his own hand to the colt's mouth and insert his fingers at the bars, Black Sand might open up. He looked at her, standing quietly, at the complete mercy of the horse she dominated while riding.

"Come, come," she scolded Black Sand. "Let go. This

72

is no time to play." The colt sniffed deeply, then snorted through blown-out nostrils.

Alec moved still closer. The colt's eyes followed him and he saw a wantonness in them that he didn't like. Black Sand might take off Pam's fingers just for the fun of it without actually meaning her any harm.

"Who will look after you better than I?" she asked the colt. "Who loves you more?"

Alec listened to her, hoping the colt would succumb to her charm. But he doubted it very much.

Alec raised his hand slowly, hoping to reach the colt's mouth without angering him. The colt's eyes gleamed brighter and Alec quickly dropped his hand. He could not do it. One wrong move from him, and the colt would sever Pam's fingers from her hand. Better to do it her way.

"Leave him be," she said, her voice maintaining its friendly, singing quality, for her words were meant for the colt as well as Alec. "It is only a game."

Yet, despite the cheerful rhythm of her words, Alec heard her swallow noisily. His heart went out to her. He wanted to leap forward to wrest her hand from the colt's mouth, but it was the last thing he should do. He could do nothing but watch and listen, wait and hope.

"I will not be able to take care of you," she told the colt. "Neither will I be able to play my flute for you. It will not be as you like it at all."

Small and fragile, she pressed herself against Black Sand, her slim neck against his, her body close to his, as if she was bound to him by a kind of inward spell. And all the while she continued to talk to him.

Alec was completely absorbed by this game she was playing with Black Sand—all the time acting as if it were not serious or critical. She seemed filled with love and trust that her horse would do her no harm. Alec was watching her face and listening to her so intently that he did not know her hand was free until she raised it to rub the colt's head.

She stroked him softly, still talking to him, while Alec waited in silence. Finally, she moved away saying, "Let's get back to work. You said you'd ride with me."

"Sure," Alec said. He wanted to ride with her, now or anytime at all.

9 • *Come to Life*

That evening Alec returned to the training barn, confused and filled with conflicting emotions. He had finished the day's work with Pam, feeling better than he had in a long time, more carefree and happy. Then he'd spent an hour in his father's office, telling him of Henry's reaction to his hiring Pam and asking for advice.

The advice had not been what he'd expected. His father agreed with Henry that Pam should go, if not for the same reasons or with the same degree of hostility.

Pam was doing her job well, his father had said. There was no fault to be found with her work, but it wasn't right to have an attractive girl working around men even there at the farm. She was one of those girls who seemed to come around so frequently in the spring, though none had ever been hired until now. She wore flamboyant clothes and flowers in her hair, even went barefoot at times; not what one would consider proper attire at a *working* horse farm. And the music coming from her apartment was enough to set his nerves on edge, electrically amplified and horrible. He'd read a lot about kids today being swept up by music, looking for ecstasy and almost going out of their heads. Now he believed it.

Another thing, his father said, Pam talked too much. The men told him she never kept still. When she wasn't talking, she was singing. No, they hadn't complained about it, he admitted to Alec. In fact, one had jokingly told him that everything she said was either funny or beautiful. But it wasn't right for her to be carrying on so while working.

"Why not?" Alec had asked.

Work, his father had replied, should be taken more seriously. It was just not normal to be so carefree. It was as if Pam put all problems in the bottom of a tack trunk, and sat on the lid laughing.

Their conversation had continued during dinner and Alec learned that his mother's reactions to Pam were, like his father's, motivated by emotion rather than logic. Girls should not compete with men in the

76

racing world, she said. It was too rough. Horse shows were much better for them. There they were treated like ladies. Girls should be more reserved and feminine. Otherwise, who would take care of the home and children?

Alec had heard these remarks made by other women, those who did not want to face the conflicts involved in challenging male supremacy and who were anxious to avoid the anti-man stigma. Now, he realized his mother was one of them, and it came as a shock to him.

His parents had continued to talk about Pam almost as if she weren't a real person, just one of today's youth, whom they judged from television and the newspapers to be very irresponsible. They were kind, wonderful parents, but Alec realized their remarks were lethal enough to poison the climate of feeling between generations. And he was further disturbed to think that they did not seem to consider him one of today's youth.

It was all very difficult to understand. He knew his parents to be fair and tolerant. They had allowed him to choose his own course in life, and had given him all the freedom any son could have asked. How else could he have shaped his life with the Black?

What had happened to them?

What had happened to Henry?

Alec entered the barn, wondering if possibly his parents and Henry were more *fearful* than angered by what Pam represented—a passion for life that went beyond obtaining material possessions, all the things they had worked so hard to get.

Right or wrong, Pam was asking questions which all of them, including himself, least wanted to hear, for such questions challenged their goals, their ideals and their conscience!

Alec went to her apartment, only to find the lights out. Quickly he descended the stairs and left the barn, knowing she was somewhere around, for her car was still there.

Night had fallen and he waited for his eyes to become adjusted to the darkness before climbing the fence and walking across the fields. There was no moon and the night was lit only by the stars.

He was almost to the edge of the woods when he heard the notes of a flute echoing in the stillness. He paused in his tracks, knowing Pam was there, somewhere ahead of him.

He had decided to tell her everything, how everyone felt about her. Then she could decide whether or not she wanted to stay. If she did, he wouldn't let her go, for his feelings had changed after spending the day with her.

He moved forward again, his steps unconsciously keeping time to the sounds of the flute. There was a smooth, steady rhythm to the beat that was beautiful in its simplicity.

He came to an abrupt stop when he saw her, for she was dancing to her music. While he watched, she leaped high on bare feet and hard, muscular legs, spun in the air and came down to fall back a pace. Then she sprang forward again, bent a knee, bounded on one leg while spinning in great whirlwinds that sent her long hair flying like great golden wings. Every inch of spine, every joint moved and flowed as she danced her own dance to her own music. Hers was a body abandoned to utter freedom. It was more than dancing,- Alec decided; it was a furious and magnificent soaring flight, performed more by the mythical god Pan than by Pam.

Finally, she collapsed to the ground, exhausted and breathing heavily. Yet even then she had an air of grace, a marvelous flare, such as comes from nature alone.

He moved forward but her eyes were closed and she did not see him. He felt that he was invading her privacy, and regretted that he had not called to her instead of stealing quietly upon her.

She was wearing a white cotton dress, sprinkled with colored blossoms. Tiny diamond earrings shone softly in the lobes of her ears. She had her arms over her head and her slender, supple body and long straight legs were stretched out in the complete relaxation of an exhausted animal.

"Hello," he said. "I would think you'd be too tired for all that."

She opened her eyes, startled to find him there.

"I didn't know I had an audience," she said with some embarrassment. "I was dancing because I'm so happy. What a fabulous, fantastic day, Alec."

"It was fun," Alec said. "I don't think I've ever been happier after a day's work."

"Me, too," she said, reaching for his hand. He took it

and sat down on the grass beside her.

Night hawks flew overhead and their gazes followed the outline of winged bodies against the sky.

"I wish I were one of them," she said. "Wings would be good for me."

"Why?" he asked. "You soar well enough without them."

"It's just that I want to see and hear everything."

"How come you're so restless?"

"I don't know," she said. "I guess I just like to go from place to place. What's the good of coming to a halt when I've so much to do?"

"But isn't it kind of a rushing thing?" Alec asked.

"I suppose so," she admitted. "But if I stay anywhere very long, it gets to be a planning thing and somehow it's wrong for me. I'm sure of that but I don't know the reasons why. It just is. I say to myself, 'I've been here long enough. I've done what I've wanted to do. I've made some money. What am I going to do with it. Save it? What for? To have what others have who've made it?' So I move on to see something else."

"Maybe you're running?" Alec put it as a question and did not say it harshly. He really wanted to know.

"Running," she repeated. "From what?"

He was going to say *life,* but realized how wrong he'd be. If she were running, as he'd suggested, she was not running away from anything but *to* something, to find something else, to discover new things, new dreams.

Alec shrugged his shoulders. "I don't know," he said.

"Maybe commitments, responsibilities." He knew the words were not really his but had come from Henry and others; yet once he'd said them he couldn't take them back.

A look of proud anger spoiled the regularity of her features. "Are you so happy with *yours?*" she asked.

"Enough," he said, giving her a surface answer. "As much as one could expect."

She raised herself on an elbow and said, "You talk around it. You leave the essentials unsaid."

"Okay," he answered, his anger mounting. "I'm one of those you despise for having made it."

She looked at him with a puzzled expression. "You're crazy," she said. "I don't think about you that way at all."

"Then why are you looking at me that way?"

"I'm not looking at you in any particular way," she said. "It's you who's looking at yourself."

"You're the one who's crazy," he answered.

She shook her head. "You're mad because you're suddenly realizing you've become more involved with the racing industry than with horses as animals."

"You're not being fair," he said, rising to his feet. "They go together. Even so, what's wrong with it?"

"Nothing. If that's the way you want it, it's great. You're doing your own thing, and that's to be envied."

"Then why are you mad?"

"I'm not mad at all. You started the whole thing by saying I was running away when I'm not. Honestly, Alec,

81

I've got my own life to live, and I don't want to copy yours or anyone else's. Neither do I want you to copy mine. I'm not trying to solve any problems. I've had too many dreams broken, but I've found that I'm not alone."

"You'll be hurt, Pam," Alec said quietly. "You and those like you."

"Hurt?" she repeated, her eyes puzzled. "How?"

"Let me tell you the way it is, the way I see it wherever I go. You're part of a whole new minority group, a movement——"

"But I don't like movements," she interrupted angrily. "What I've been talking about can only be handled by people like you and me understanding each other, not by *movements*."

"Others see it as a group thing nevertheless," Alec continued. "Maybe it's what you say it is but they see it as a revolution, one whose purpose they don't understand, but a revolution anyway. They'll put it down forcefully if necessary. Let me tell you how Henry feels about your working here, and even my parents. It'll give you an idea what I mean."

When he had finished telling her how they felt, he concluded by saying, "It's up to you. Do you want to stay?"

"What about you?" she asked. "How do *you* feel? Do you want me to stay?" She swallowed noisily and her voice trembled. Alec realized she was very near to tears.

"You know I want you here," he said.

"The funny thing is that I thought your mother and father liked me," she said finally. "They've been so nice."

"They *are* nice people," Alec said. "They just don't understand the way it is with you. It'll take time, but they'll come around."

"And Henry? What about him?"

"He's something else again," Alec admitted, "but he'll be at the track, not here."

"On television he looks like one of those wonderful old men," she said. "Mature, understanding, very gentle and kind, one who has a way with kids as well as young horses."

"Well, he always has been that way," Alec said. "But now he's frightened of something he doesn't understand, like a lot of others."

"Even so, why build walls instead of bridges?" she asked.

Alec shrugged his shoulders. "Maybe for the same reason I got mad at you a few minutes ago," he said. "Because what you said of me was true, and I didn't like to hear it."

"But you're not mad any longer?"

"No," he said, taking her hand. "Say what you like and if I disagree with you I'll tell you so, but I won't get mad any more. I promise."

She laughed, suddenly her old self again. He met her eyes squarely, to convince himself as well as her, that there was no anger, no bitterness within him. He had only to look at her to know that it would be impossible for her to betray a friend, to lie about her emotions or to break a promise. She would always play it straight, regardless of the consequences to herself; there was no phoniness within her. He must be that way, too, if they were to be more than friends.

"I have to go back tomorrow," he said. "Will you stay here, Pam?"

"Yes," she said, meeting his eyes. "I want to stay very much."

"Then it's all settled," he said. "Now we can talk about us."

10 • *Box Office Bonanza*

When Alec arrived at Aqueduct the following afternoon, the stable area was quiet. It was just after twelve o'clock and there was little for caretakers to do. A few late-working horses were being cooled out and walked monotonously in circles.

The quiet was suddenly broken by the crackling of the loudspeaker system as a message came over it for one of the trainers. Alec jumped at the noise and decided he wasn't as calm about facing Henry as he had thought.

Reaching the tack room, he looked inside, expecting to find Henry. Instead, Deb, their night caretaker, was stretched out on the cot, reading the *Morning Tele-graph.*

"Hey," Alec greeted him. "Where's Henry?"

The man put down his newspaper. "He's gone up front, Alec. Said he wanted to watch the races today."

"Everything okay here?"

"Yeah, sure."

Deb was as old as Henry and perhaps more dependable when it came to caring for horses. He was a true racetracker, having gone from track to track all his life, caring only for his beloved charges and the day's eating money. Most important to Alec, he got along with the Black, who allowed few people to approach him. A good caretaker was equal in value to a good horse. It was impossible to have one without the other, just as it was impossible for Henry and Alec to be with the Black every moment.

Alec went to the Black's stall and found the stallion resting in a far corner. He realized how much his horse would have enjoyed being at the farm, if only for a short time. The Black was a lover of freedom. He thrived on blowing wind and green grass. Although Alec walked him every day at Aqueduct, allowing him to pick grass, it was not enough.

Alec remained with the Black a long while. Horsemen who loved their horses were all alike, he thought. Each was filled with the same certainty that the horse he loved was the fastest, bravest, strongest, kindest and smartest.

It was 12:30 when Alec entered the towering glass-fronted stands and joined a steady stream of people. He felt the electric air of the race track flowing from one person to another but he felt very much alone, unattached and anonymous. He did not belong with the fans but on the track itself.

"Telly. Morning Telegraph. Telly," shouted the gravelly voices of men, hawking their papers and programs. "Girl jock rides today. Here y'are, read all about her. Get the winners. *Telly. Morning Telly."*

Alec bought a paper, interested in learning which of the girl jockeys was riding that day. There had been several during the past month, but they hadn't done much except to get a lot of publicity.

Glancing at the paper, Alec learned that Becky Moore was riding in the first race. He quickened his pace. Weather clear, track fast and a girl riding against men! No wonder there was such a large crowd, with everyone scurrying to reach his seat before post time.

Walking across the lower lobby, Alec found himself comparing Becky Moore with Pam. Both loved horses but they were at the opposite ends of the pole in every other way. He'd known Becky for the two years she'd been working around the track. She was shy and modest almost to the point of embarrassment. None of the men ever got mad at Becky; in fact, no one had really thought of her as a girl until she'd applied for her jockey's license and was racing.

That was the way Becky had wanted it, Alec decided. Quietly, unobtrusively she had worked her way through

87

the ranks until one afternoon she appeared on a race horse as a girl jockey. It had been as simple as that, but very well planned and executed. No friction between male and female, no problems, no outspokenness. She'd been there and yet not there, all the while very ambitious, knowing where she was going and having her sights set on big-time racing.

Everything Pam stood for was not for Becky. While Pam concealed nothing about herself or her motives, Becky by her shyness and gentleness concealed a hardness that would be fierce in open competition and catch most male jockeys unprepared. Becky would do all right today and any other day, Alec decided.

Arriving at a closed door on the far side of the lobby, Alec showed his horseman's pass to a track policeman and went inside.

Within the confines of the vast grandstand it was quiet, almost peaceful, compared to the commotion that was going on in the four tiers of stands overhead. Alec walked down a long corridor, passing rooms and offices and not stopping until he reached the Jockeys' Room. Since he wasn't racing, he wasn't allowed inside, but he stood in the open doorway.

"Hey, Alec," one rider called to him. "We've got a girl-driver on our hands today."

"So I've heard."

"Becky's no girl," another said. "She's a tomboy. Didya' ever see her in a dress?"

"No, but she's still a girl, and she rides like a girl,"

88

the first jockey answered. "Got good hands but no arms. All she can do is sit there and steer. Isn't that right, Alec?"

"Steering a horse is pretty important," Alec said.

"Yeah, but it takes arm strength to handle a horse in tight quarters."

"And let's see her con a horse to run when he doesn't want to run," another rider said.

"When the day comes I can't ride better than a girl, I'll quit," the first jockey said.

"Me too," a veteran agreed. "I've been ridin' fifteen years and I learn something new every day, so what do I have to worry about a girl for? Don't get me wrong," he added. "I like Becky. Everybody likes Becky."

"If everybody likes Becky," another rider quipped, "what's she afraid of? Why does she have that big dog in her car? A signal from her and he'd eat you alive."

"She may be a tomboy, but she's still a girl," someone said. "She must feel safer having him around."

"Anyway," the first jockey said, turning back to Alec. "These girl jocks aren't for real. Right, Alec? They're just a box-office attraction, a bonanza. It won't last. Sooner or later the novelty of seeing girl jocks on the card will wear off and that will be the last of them."

"It could be," Alec said.

"Meanwhile, God bless them and keep them safe," someone in the back said.

"And us too," another said. "Women drivers make me nervous. They cause pileups."

Alec continued down the corridor, heading for the

elevator that would take him to the press section, where he knew he'd find Henry. It afforded the best view of the track and the trainer always watched the races from there.

Alec thought of what the jockeys had said. It was true that added danger was involved when girls rode against men—not that girl riders weren't as capable as men in handling their horses, but women jockeys could upset the style and strategy of male riders. Most men would think twice, as he would, before doing anything that might endanger the life of a girl. But in racing you couldn't afford to think twice. If you did, you might get killed yourself. Steel-shod hoofs made a pretty sound on a track but not on a guy's head.

What the male jockeys hadn't mentioned, though Alec knew it was very much on their minds, was the fact that girl riders threatened their earning power. They feared a greatly reduced income if girl jockeys successfully invaded their ranks. Many of the men were married and it was not easy for them to support their families on what they made. They had to pay out a twenty per cent commission to their agents plus Guild dues and valet, travel and equipment expenses. It was not all roses, this being a professional jockey.

Apprentice riders, which included all the girls racing at this time, were allowed ten pounds below the weight assigned to their mount until they had ridden five winners; then they were allowed five pounds to an additional thirty winners. Since weight was the name of the game, good apprentices were always in demand, and a trainer would use any girl rider he thought capable of handling his horses. That would put a lot of little men off horses.

Reaching the elevator, Alec greeted the newsmen gathered there. When the car arrived he went to the back, grateful for all the talk and activity that had kept him from thinking of his forthcoming confrontation with Henry. He didn't intend to change his mind about Pam's staying at Hopeful Farm, regardless of Henry's wrath.

Quickly, the elevator rose to the topmost tier of the great stands, the height of a ten-story building. Alec followed the others out, walked down a corridor to the front of the stands and entered the press section.

There was nothing within the large room to obstruct the view of the track and infield below, but Alec's eyes did not go to the vastness of open space before him. Instead, his gaze passed over the men milling around the room, waiting for the call to the post for the first race of the day. He saw Henry, standing in a far corner, all by himself.

Alec moved past the clicking typewriters and teletype machines, wondering what the outcome of this meeting would be. Had it actually come to making a choice between Henry and Pam? He couldn't, *wouldn't* believe it.

11 • *Man to Man*

Henry turned away when he saw Alec. He looked out the window, his strong beaky nose prominent against the sky.

"Hi," Alec said.

Henry turned back and studied Alec with a patient and reserved air. "How'd things go at the farm?" he asked.

"Fine," Alec said. "The two-year-olds look great, especially Black Sand."

Henry waited for an explanation as to what had been done about the *girl*. When it was not forthcoming, he asked, "Did you let her go?"

"No, I didn't."

Henry spread his nostrils and filled his huge chest with fresh air coming through the open window. His eyes did not waver from Alec's, yet they disclosed his astonishment at this break between them.

"Why not?" Henry asked. "I told you I wouldn't have her around."

"She's better with the horses than I thought she'd be," Alec said. "I couldn't let her go."

Henry turned abruptly away to look at the horses parading to the post. He watched them a moment, then his gaze returned to Alec.

"I don't like having these arguments with you," he said. "We've been friends too long and have too much at stake to split over a girl. I know you don't like some of the things I've said, but you've got to understand that girls have no place in this game. Give them a single opening and they cause all kinds of problems. I've been around long enough to know."

"She's working at the farm, not here," Alec said. He was aware that Henry was watching him closely, as if making a final assessment before coming to a decision. Alec hoped his face disclosed his determination not to change his mind. He was not going to be intimidated by Henry's threat to leave. The old trainer had as much to lose by it as he did.

"You must have good reason for wanting to keep her," Henry said, playing for time.

"I told you she's very capable. Go see her. Judge for

93

yourself. You can't talk about somebody you don't even know."

"No, I'll stay here," Henry said. "But besides her being capable . . . I mean, you must be pretty keen on her, aren't you?"

"Yes, there's that too," Alec admitted.

"I thought as much," Henry said. He rested his massive frame against the window sill, his mouth spreading in a wide smile, as if now he understood what Alec's defiance was all about.

"I must be getting pretty old not to have figured that one out long before this," Henry continued. "You've got every right to be attracted to a pretty girl. Perhaps, it'll do you some good, make you less tense and easier to get along with. We've had lots of arguments lately and some unpleasantness.

"Okay, Alec," he concluded quickly, having made up his mind. "I'll agree to her staying. Just have your *fun* up there, all you want. But don't bring her down here."

Alec's cheeks stiffened and there was a surge of redness beneath his tan. He was angered by the trainer's suggestive remarks. It was another instance of Henry's thinking in terms of his own youth. He would not or could not understand that relationships between boys and girls *had* changed since his day. No more than Henry could understand what it was like for Alec to be with Pam as a person, another human being—not just a pretty girl.

However, Alec decided not to say anything in reply. It was enough that Pam would remain at Hopeful Farm.

94

He turned to the window to watch the horses going to the post for the first race of the day.

The race was to be run over a distance of a mile, beginning in the chute on the far side of the track. There would be four furlongs to go to the far turn, two more going around it and then two furlongs for home. The race was for maidens—horses which had never won a race—with a purse of $5,000.

The area around Alec and Henry became crowded as newsmen jammed close. One man said, "Becky Moore was mobbed when she left her dressing room to go to the paddock, but Mike Costello was looking after her. It seems he's appointed himself her bodyguard or boyfriend or something."

"Anything but boyfriend," another reporter said. "Becky doesn't want any boyfriends. Besides, Mike's too old for her. He'd be more like her adopted father."

Alec watched Mike Costello, one of the most experienced jockeys in the business, riding to the post beside Becky, looking out for her every foot of the way. He was standing in his stirrup irons, talking to her, when they reached the gate. Becky looked very poised, as usual; there was nothing in her slight figure to disclose that she was a girl or, for that matter, that she needed any assistance from Mike Costello.

Becky's horse, a four-year-old mare, was being led into Number 5 starting stall. Becky had finished fourth with this same horse a week ago, and now the mare was coming back in a race where she belonged and would be twice as tough to beat. She was one of the two favorites.

Becky pulled down her goggles, ready to go.

"She's going to win this one," a sports columnist said.

Henry answered, "From what I've seen of her, the boys have nothing to worry about. A few greedy people, including some trainers I know, are exploiting her for the sake of publicity."

"Maybe so," the columnist agreed. "She's never raced more than six furlongs before and this mile will be a long trip for her."

Alec's gaze left Becky to move to the other jockeys. It was a large field of ten, and the majority of them were apprentice riders like Becky. There would be a lot of jamming, and he wondered if any of them would give way to her.

In the outside stall, Number 10, Alec saw a horse jump up and down while a crewman tried to bring him under control. The jockey was Mario Santos, the leading apprentice rider at the track with twenty-six winners. He was 103 pounds of Latin fury on a five-foot, five-inch frame. The nineteen-year-old Mario had told Alec he'd stopped growing at the age of fifteen in his home island of Puerto Rico. He had no weight problems and Alec, watching him eat pound cake and candy in the track kitchen, could readily believe it. Mario was not one to take care of a girl, as Mike Costello did. Neither were any of the other riders. All were hungry for money and success, and therefore very aggressive.

The front doors flew open, and over the track's loudspeaker system came the announcer's call, *"They're off!"*

12 • *Maiden Race*

At first, Alec saw nothing but a blur of multi-colored silks, then the outside horse emerged. Mario Santos' horse may have been jumping up and down in the gate, but he'd broken fast. Becky was somewhere in the middle of the pack. Alec found her red silks and kept his binoculars on her.

She sat very still and well balanced in her saddle, allowing the mare to settle into racing stride without hurrying or worrying her. Faster and faster moved the packed field, as if no force on earth could stop it. Heads bobbed together. Bodies strained, shoulder to shoulder.

Alec knew the fear that came at such a time, the difficulty of keeping balance in the desperate jamming and wobbling, the hard lessons learned from jockeys who elbowed you, pinched you against the fence and between horses.

It was easier for the riders now that the first mad brush had been won and lost. They were well away from the gate, moving from the chute into the backstretch, with a little over a quarter of a mile to go before reaching the far turn, the only turn in the race.

Alec found Becky again. She was rocking in her saddle, urging her mount on with hands and legs. Mike Costello was alongside, his head bobbing with hers. Neither had an inch over the other, neither gave way. But Alec suspected that was the way Mike wanted it. Whatever the reason, Mike was taking care of Becky every step of the way. Together they moved through the pack and neared the front-running leaders.

They swept into the turn with blinding speed and Becky began using her whip as she guided her mount away from Mike Costello and over to the rail. Alec saw Mike start to go with her but then his horse began bearing out and, for a few seconds, he had to pay strict attention to what he was doing. When Mike got his horse straightened out again, Becky was somewhere in the pack.

Alec had a good idea of the thoughts going through Mike's head at this time. *Where is she? Is she going to do something foolish that could hurt herself or someone else?*

98

Alec shifted his binoculars from Mike to Becky, finding her close to the rail amidst four other hard-running horses.

"She's taken off on her own," Henry said, "and the heat's on! Now we'll find out what she can do without Mike squiring her around the track." He sounded gleeful, as if expecting the worst.

Alec kept his binoculars on Becky. "She's tough," he said, "and she's pulling out all the stops today."

Henry answered, "She'll wilt like any girl would when the heat's turned on."

The horses came off the turn and entered the homestretch with two furlongs, a quarter of a mile, to go. Becky was on the rail with Mario Santos racing beside her. Two horses were directly in front of them, also running as a team. Mario was hand riding while Becky was making good use of her whip, flaying her horse and trying to break through.

"Mario will never let her off the rail," Henry said. "He's no gentleman."

Alec watched Mario, knowing the popular apprentice would stay behind the two leaders until it was time to swing outside and loop them. Mario had a lot of horse left under him, and he was taking advantage of the situation by keeping Becky, on the favorite, pinched against the rail. Mario was strong and able to use his strength to assist his horse without resorting to his whip until necessary. For now, he was content to wait.

A mounting crescendo of cheers greeted the horses as

they flashed below in the stretch drive. Alec kept his binoculars on the leaders. Even under ideal circumstances, it was easy to miss dramatic details—a bump, a thrown shoe, careless riding—that won or lost a race. He saw Becky switch the whip from left to right hand, smoothly without any loss of rhythm. In the face of her flaying whip Mario gave way a little but still didn't give her any room to get through.

The horse in front of Becky was tiring and she rushed for a narrow opening he left on the rail. The tiring horse bore in sharply just as Becky neared the opening and she was squeezed against the rail. Alec knew her leg was hard against the fence and the horse was burning his hide on it. Yet Becky continued to urge her mount on, her whip rising and falling with no letup.

"She's squeezing through!" Alec shouted incredulously.

"She'll quit," Henry said. "She'll never make it."

Mario Santos saw Becky getting through on the inside and went to his whip. His mount jumped at the belts of leather against his hide, and raced quickly around the two tiring leaders. Becky had broken through on the rail and there was nothing in her mount's path! She continued whipping with her right hand as her horse raced furiously for the wire. Mario, rocking in his saddle, caught Becky as her mount faltered under the staccato beat of her whip.

Becky moved up again, regaining the inches lost to Mario's horse, and went to the front. The stands were in an uproar as the two horses and their apprentice riders scuffed and scrubbed with hands and feet, trying to get the last ounce of speed from their mounts.

Becky switched her whip to the left side without loss of stride. Mario was whipping with his right, and the horses were hide-scraping as they came down to the finish. Again, Becky's horse faltered and lost a few inches to Mario's horse. Heads bobbed together, noses stretched out, striving, reaching for the finish wire.

"She's tiring! She's lost it!" Henry said.

Alec didn't answer. At a time like this, he didn't think; he just watched. It would be over in a final jump.

Mario continued driving hard, his horse inching away from Becky's. But Becky wasn't out of the race, not yet. She refused to give up *and miraculously her horse came on again!* In a single, mighty leap she ranged up boldly alongside Mario. Then another stride came as swiftly, and she went under the wire, winner by a head!

Henry was the first to turn away from the window. "Big deal," he told a reporter. "She gets a horse that's pounds the best and manages not to fall off."

Few newsmen agreed with him; the consensus was that Becky had ridden the kind of race any man would have wanted for himself. She had beaten Mario Santos, New York's leading apprentice, at his own kind of game, riding with head, hands and legs in a brilliant, driving finish. Becky had raced from the status of something on the order of a sideshow attraction to a main-ring performer in one grueling duel.

101

"She'll be getting more mounts from now on," a reporter said. "She's tough."

"I'll agree with you on that," Henry said. "Sweet, little Becky surprised everybody, but it won't happen again. There'll be no more squiring her around, like Mike did today. The boys will know what to expect from now on."

Alec followed Henry across the room. He was eager to call Pam and tell her that she could remain at Hopeful Farm.

As Alec went to a telephone, Henry said, "If you're calling your girl friend, tell her you won't be around for a while. I've got a new schedule worked out for us. We're leaving for the West Coast tomorrow and racing at Hollywood Park on Saturday. It'll be a month before we're back."

Alec didn't answer. It was no time to reveal his great disappointment at not being able to see Pam next week as planned. But he knew she would be there when he got back. Despite her great love for freedom, she'd never leave the horses without seeing him. However, a month away was a long while—and he didn't know how much time he had left to be with Pam.

13 · *A Champion's Way*

The following day the Black was flown to California, and those who went with him—Alec, Henry and Deb—felt as only people who are in the entourage of a great champion can. When they arrived at the Los Angeles airport, a large crowd, including the press, was there to meet them. They had gathered to look at the horse many of them knew only from newspapers and magazines and television. They peered into the plane and watched as he was transferred to a waiting van which took him to Hollywood Park, four miles away.

The week that followed was unlike any other period

Alec had ever spent. He found Californians different from the fans back east, where horsemen and the public alike accepted the Black as champion without question. This was a "show-me" crowd, one seemingly determined to topple him from his pedestal to prove the superiority of their horses over those from the East. Never before had Alec thought of the Black as belonging to any one particular section of the country.

The Black was ready, Alec knew, to prove his greatness to them. There was not a pound of surplus flesh on him anywhere, and his form on the track matched the heroic proportions of his great body. Soon after his arrival he worked six furlongs in the blazing time of 1:08. Then the morning before his first race he was blown-out three furlongs in :32, both under the strongest kind of pull by Alec.

Back at the stable, Henry said, "I hope those times aren't going to scare the others off. He might be racing all by himself tomorrow."

The next day a large field of twelve horses went post-ward against the Black in the Sunset Handicap, a mile-and-a-half race over the turf course. But the great champion might have been racing alone, as Henry had antici-pated. Coming into the homestretch of the long race, he was racing only his shadow while the others plodded along some fifty lengths in the rear. At the end he was running with the breathtaking speed of a sprinter, with Alec sitting still in the saddle.

The Black came back to the winner's circle with his

tail in the air. His time on the electric board read 2:23, faster than any horse in the world had ever gone before, perhaps a record never to be equaled!

The spectators rose to their feet in a standing ovation, and Alec knew that his horse had proved to one and all that he was truly a great champion.

Henry picked up first money of some $66,000 and told Alec that, though they were well on their way, this was only the beginning. He meant that they would be winning more and more purse money, Alec knew, for there were several very rich races ahead of them. Once more, Alec thought of Pam and her interest in horses simply for the love and enjoyment of them. Despite the fact that he knew it was his job as well as Henry's to earn enough money to operate Hopeful Farm, he was sensitive to the trainer's continued emphasis on purses rather than the electrifying beauty of the Black's performance.

Californians' attitude toward the Black, backside as well as in the stands, changed overnight. His world-shattering record, made on their track, won their hearts. Now he belonged to them as well as to Easterners. They watched every move he made, and Alec could no longer call even the nights his own. He became resigned to people following him and his horse everywhere, around the barns and on the track, hanging over rails, watching the Black work and never quite believing their stopwatches. The Black took such giant strides when he ran alone in his workouts that one was never truly aware of his great speed without a watch on him.

Another large field of ten horses went against him in his second start a week later. He carried a heavy impost of 140 pounds and again made a shambles of a good field by winning the Los Angeles Handicap in track-record time.

Henry pocketed winner's money of $54,000 and told Alec, "I knew the weight wouldn't bother him none over seven-eighths of a mile. He might have had some trouble with them at a mile and over, but not at seven furlongs."

"Then why'd you make so much fuss when he was assigned that weight?" Alec asked.

Henry grinned. "You wouldn't want them to think I was *happy* about it, would you?"

"No, I guess not," Alec answered. It was Henry's strategy never to let anyone think he was satisfied with the imposts put on the Black. He was as sensitive as an apothecary's scale to weights. In the past he had withdrawn the Black when he believed the weight assignment was excessive. He wouldn't do that in California, Alec decided. Henry was out to bank all the purse money he could get his hands on, and in as short a time as possible.

During the weeks that followed, the Black went postward three more times and had the track almost to himself. The trainers at Hollywood Park had acknowledged his invincibility—not in words, but in an even stronger way. They kept their horses in the barns. Only a few were willing even to race for second money; they did not want to embarrass their owners or themselves by suffering humiliating defeats.

The Black carried 140 pounds in each race, giving up to thirty-five pounds to the few horses who ventured forth to race him. These contests were more exhibitions than races, and the fans watched them as such, their applause swelling as the Black came back, their eyes leaving him only to check the times posted on the electric board. They realized that, even under the strongest kind of restraint, he had been very close to lowering more records.

The hero worship given the Black was completely out of control, Alec knew, but neither he nor Henry could do anything about it.

"Don't let all this go to your head," he told the Black in the privacy of his stall, the only place he could ever find to be alone with him, and then only with both halves of the door closed. He doubted that all the clamor had any effect on his horse; the danger of overconfidence rested with those who took care of him.

The Black belonged to everybody in the stable, and this was their hour of triumph as well as the champion's. The Black was a super horse, and they stood proudly beside him, sharing his fame.

Yet it was not easy for them to have such a horse in their stable. It took more endurance, more stamina than most people realized. Every casual remark made by any of them was repeated and published for the world to read. Each person was the subject of intense criticism as well as envy. Few people seemed to know that even a great horse could be beaten by a misstep on the track, a stable accident, bad racing luck, even a slight cold or an off day. A loving but severe public would tolerate no excuse, even the thousand or more trivial ones that could defeat the Black.

Henry was too old to hope that he would ever have another champion like the Black and Alec doubted that the trainer would want one. Henry was more irritable than ever. He had taken just about all he could from the public, from newsmen, even from his fellow horsemen at the track.

Alec glanced at the two huge wads of cotton Henry had placed in the Black's ears so the loud music in the adjoining stable would be muted and not disturb him. The stable kept a radio tuned to a station specializing in loud, popular music. It blared away all day long. Fighting mad, Henry had asked the trainer to tone it down or put an end to it. The man had shaken his head and replied that everyone in the area liked the music, including his horses; it helped them get used to the commotion and the band music on race days. It was good for them.

The trainer was one of the many promising young horsemen racing in California, and when Henry angrily told him it would drive his animals crazy, citing his own age-old experience with horses, the young trainer had answered, "Times have changed, Pops. You're just not with it any more, even if you do have a big horse in your stable."

Alec pulled the Black's head down to him. He didn't think the loud music bothered the stallion, but he'd left the cotton in anyway. The Black might be sensitive to noise, but he was intelligent as well, and it should not upset him. Maybe he even liked it, as Alec did. Some of the records were those Alec had heard Pam play, and they brought her very close to him.

Soon they would return to Aqueduct, where life— even with a champion—was easier than in Hollywood Park. He would go to the farm immediately to see Pam. He was beginning to realize how much she meant to him. Somehow, he must convince her to stay on.

The following week—with another triumphant race behind him and an additional $43,000 added to his winnings—the Black and his entourage returned to Aqueduct.

14 • "I Give You Arcturus"

It was late evening, the day of his return to Aqueduct, when Alec drove down the country road leading to Hopeful Farm. Reaching the main gate, he stopped the car and climbed the board fence. He paused on the top rail.

The fields and lower woods lay in ghostly silence before him, draped in a lightly veiled mist. Sounds carried easily across the silence. He heard the sharp neighs of mares, followed almost instantly by the nickerings of foals and the clatter of hoofs.

He had called Pam from New York, and had told her

he'd be up right away. She had said that, if it was after
dark, he would find her with Black Sand at a spring-fed
pool they both knew well.

Alec jumped to the ground and walked across the pasture, his arms swinging loosely against his thin but hard
frame. Like a smooth-gaited animal he moved quickly
through the night mist, his nostrils sniffing the scents of
pasture grasses and the warm bodies of horses. He could
see the dark figures of broodmares and their suckling
foals. The joy and excitement of being home and seeing
Pam again grew with every stride.

His gaze followed the cleanliness of the white fences
and well-cared-for fields. Unfortunately, Henry was right,
he decided; they needed to win big purses to keep the
farm going. It was not something on which they could
lose money and charge off the loss on their tax returns,
as did wealthy sportsmen who bred and raced horses for
the fun of it. While such people were important, they
were not the backbone of racing, as many thought. No,
it was horsemen like Henry who carried most of the
burden, and they waged war against each other to make a
profitable living for themselves and the thousands they
employed at farms and tracks.

Alec wondered if Pam would ever accept such materi-
alistic goals and remain with him. She was still trying to
make this the best of all possible worlds, while he was
willing to accept it as the only world he had and make
the best of it. Maybe they could reach a compromise.

The mist lifted and he could see the starry sky. It was

111

a beautiful night. Peaceful. Healthy. Friendly. He climbed another fence and broke into a run, breathing deeply the air that was so cool and light.

"I'm back, Pam!" he called aloud, and then laughed because he knew she was still too far away to hear him.

Finally, tall trees loomed before him, like arrows aimed at the night sky. He slowed to a walk as he entered the woods that were part of the lower field. The light from the stars filtered through the beeches and elms and pines, making it easy for him to follow the path. He came to a large pool, fed by a spring, where he found her.

She was sitting on the ground, her back against the trunk of a tree and her head turned toward Black Sand drinking at the pool. Alec remained where he was, a short distance away. Her face was as he had visualized it so often during the past month. He saw her profile in the whitish light from the stars, her features chiseled with perfect precision.

Yet she appeared so much smaller, lighter, weaker than he remembered. Why then had he thought of her as having so much strength? Was it that she always met his eyes, when he talked to her? That she never lied about her emotions or broke a promise? That she always played it straight?

Alec took a step forward, and she heard him before the colt did. In a single movement, as quick and supple as the stretching of an animal, she was on her feet and had her arms around him.

Holding her, Alec said, "I didn't mean to startle you."

"You didn't." She laughed. "After all, I was expecting you." She pushed him away to get a better look.

"Well . . . ?" Alec asked finally, his gaze fixed on hers. He knew she was appraising him, as he had her, after a month's absence.

"You look great," she said, "very rugged and fit."

"I worked hard, if that's what you mean. We did a lot of racing in a short time."

She squinted back at him. "I've been working hard, too."

"And you look great, too," Alec said.

Her tawny hair, parted in the middle, fell long to either side of her face. A light cotton dress outlined her trim, supple body.

"How are the colts?" he asked.

"They're working well," she answered, "especially Black Sand." She glanced at the colt grazing nearby. "He's faster than ever. Things have worked out pretty well between us."

"I'm happy for you and for him," Alec said, taking her in his arms again.

"And for yourself too?"

"Yes, I'm happy for me too."

"But it was not all to the good in California, was it?" she asked after a moment. "You look a little . . . well, *tense* I guess."

Alec did not answer right away. He didn't want to tell her that the only purpose of the trip had been to make as much money for Hopeful Farm as possible. This, added to the normal strain of racing the Black, had put him under a lot of pressure which he still felt.

Finally, as if in some kind of self-justification, he said, "The Black did everything he was asked to do, but it wasn't easy. He sprinted and went a distance. He raced on all kind of tracks—slow, muddy and fast. He carried as much weight as they put on his back, and we won every time."

She was silent a moment, then said, "I'm happy you won every time. That's important to you, isn't it?"

"It is because it's our business, Pam," he said quietly. "We race horses for money—a dubious honor I'll admit, but the money is *real*, and we need it to run this place."

"Sure, I understand," she said. "But now you're home and you don't have to think about it anymore, not for a while anyway."

They walked over to the spring-fed pool, kneeled down and drank cold water from the hollow of their hands. Then they stretched out on the grass, side by side, and looked up at the stars.

The warm earth felt good beneath Alec's back and slowly he felt his tense muscles relax. The feeling stayed with him and he took Pam's hand.

"I give you Arcturus, Pam," he said, pointing to a big, bright-orange star directly above them. "See it up there? It's yours."

She laughed, very pleased, and said, "Thank you, sir."

While they were watching, a falling star streaked through the southern sky, its golden tail fanning out like

114

a searchlight before disappearing altogether.

She turned her head toward him and said in genuine alarm, "I don't want to fall like that, Alec, not until I'm all I can be."

Surprised by her seriousness, he said, "You'll never fall, Pam, not you. But even if you did, I'd be there to catch you." Then, seeing that she was truly afraid, he took her in his arms and kissed her.

"I believe you *would* catch me," she said, her face pressed against his, "because it takes life to love life. And I am you as you are you as you are me."

"That's a very nice thought," he said.

Her thoughts and comments had a way of scattering in all directions, Alec decided. Sometimes they were clear, sometimes cloudy, but always interesting.

He kept his arms around her and finally they talked of her world, the one she was trying to make the best of all worlds.

"It's insane the way it is now," she said. "Everybody looking for something and desperate. Who are we? What are we? Can we make it? Rush, rush, rush. Do something. Accomplish something. Don't be left out. No stopping, no quiet. Make up your mind. This is bad. This is good. Fussing, feuding, fuming. Preaching and pointing fingers. Dividing people into *us* and *them*. It's all so destructive, Alec! All such a phony substitute for being satisfied with one's own self, one's own being, and one's own life."

Alec thought she had finished, only to hear her add in

115

a voice barely audible, "There's a time to be still, I think, to enjoy the pleasure of being alone, like now, like it is with us."

"Then why don't you stay here?" he asked seriously. "Why your great need to move on, if you believe all you said?"

"I don't know *why*." She paused a moment, thoughtful, and then said, "Something tells me to go on and see as much as I can. Do you believe in ESP or second sight, Alec?"

He did not answer right away, not until she raised her head from the ground and prodded him. "Well, do you?"

"I've never thought much about it," he said. "I suppose it's possible. The brain is still pretty much unknown space."

She lay back in his arms again. "Anyway," she said, "for some reason I can't explain, time seems desperately short and precious to me, so I try to pack in a lot of things."

"You're being crazy again, like you were when you saw the falling star. The only reason you move on, Pam, is that's the way you want it. It's your thing. You like people. You like to be on the go."

"Yes," she said, laughing, suddenly her gay self once more. "I like people despite what I said about them before. There are always times when I hit it off with somebody, as I do with you. It makes up for a lot. You know, Alec, sometimes it's harder to be free than not free. True love is giving up that which you love most, if

116

need be, when the time comes."

"I wouldn't know," Alec said sullenly. He didn't like being included among those with whom she got along. He wanted to be very special. He wanted their being together *to last*. "I haven't yet had to give up anything I love," he added after a long pause.

"But you will," she said. "It happens to everybody."

Once more Alec found her strange blue eyes looking deep into him and he had the feeling that she saw past him and beyond. Fearful that he would lose her, he tightened his arms about her and she put her head in the hollow of his neck.

15 • One x One

The next morning, soon after first light, Alec learned that Black Sand was ready to be raced. He watched Pam break the strapping, big-boned colt from the gate with astonishing smoothness for one who was still in the growing, awkward phase of his life. The workout was a test of speed and Pam rode him as if she were indeed in a race.

Alec knew the colt was listening to her because he had an ear cocked as he swept by, his every stride one of marvelous control and training. How had Pam accomplished so much with him in only a month? He watched her guide the colt easily from the middle of the track over

118

to the rail and then into the first turn. Black Sand did not drift out as so many young horses did, but hung onto the rail as if it were a part of him.

Alec recalled only too well that of all the two-year-olds in the barn, Black Sand had been the most difficult to ride. He had trusted no one and, considering the mistreatment he'd suffered as a yearling in the hands of his previous owner, it was understandable. Still, despite all their patience and care, they had been able to do little with him until Pam had come along.

Alec kept his binoculars on Black Sand as he swept down the backstretch. There was no doubt the colt ran for the sheer love of racing, even against himself. Pam was only a tawny blur on his back, sitting very still as if hypnotized by her mount's blinding speed. Black Sand was perfectly balanced, hardly aware of the light weight he carried, yet obviously responding to Pam's hands. He drove relentlessly into the far turn and came around it to enter the homestretch, his strides never faltering in their smooth triple racing beat.

Alec did not have to look at his stopwatch to know how fast they were going. The quarter mile had been run just slightly under :25 and the half, faster still, in :48. Both were better than any trainer could have asked of a two-year-old at this stage of his development. Black Sand could begin his racing campaign immediately and next year, at three, if nothing happened to him, he would be strong enough to go on to the classic distances of the Kentucky Derby, the Preakness, and the Belmont,

119

for he was bred for stamina as well as speed.

When Pam returned with Black Sand, Alec said, "You were right. He's ready. I'll take him with me when I go."

"I'll miss him," she said, her arms wrapped around the colt's neck.

Alec recalled Henry's warning, not to let Pam near Aqueduct. Yet he heard himself ask, "Why don't you ride down with us? You haven't had a day off since you got here."

She hugged the colt again, and Alec saw the indecision in her face. "I don't know," she said. "What about Henry?"

"I'll think of something," Alec said, although he didn't quite know what it would be or how he would handle it. "I've got three days before going back," he added. "I'll think of something."

The three days went by quickly for Alec. He learned what Pam had meant the first night when she talked of their oneness. It was a closeness between two people he had never known before, the giving of one's self rather than the thinking of one's self. They rode together, worked together, and there were many hours when they just walked in the grass in their bare feet, something she couldn't believe he'd never done before at the farm. And never before, too, had he been aware of each sound, each touch, everything he looked at, every passing minute, day and night.

"You know, Pam," he told her the night before leaving for Aqueduct. "I know it sounds wild, but I've never been so happy." He meant it with all his heart and, for some reason, he felt it necessary to tell her even though he was sure she knew. Was it that time suddenly seemed desperately short and precious to him, that he feared he might go to the barn one morning and find her gone?

"I called Henry and told him I was bringing Black Sand," he said. "I didn't mention anything about your coming."

"I'm glad you didn't because I'm not," she answered. "I've decided it wouldn't work, Alec. It would mean too much unpleasantness for all of us. Besides, it's . . ."

"It would be a change of scene for you," Alec interrupted deliberately, afraid that she'd been going to say it was time for her to move on. "You wouldn't have to stay long. You might even like it. I race the Black on Saturday. I'd like you to see him, Pam. You never have except on television. He's different in the flesh. It's an important race, one of the toughest for him. Please . . ."

Her blue eyes searched his, squinting as she laughed. "It does sound like fun," she said, "and I would like to see you race the Black. It's something I've always wanted to do. Okay, I'll be down Saturday, if just to watch."

"But don't go away afterward," Alec warned. "I'll expect you at the barn."

"All right," she promised. "I'll be there."

Alec put his arm around her waist and they walked through the night together.

16 • *Five in a Row*

At four-fifteen, the following Saturday afternoon, Alec
rode the Black into the starting gate at Aqueduct. The
band had stopped playing and the post parade was over.
The horses were at the post for the running of the
Manhattan Handicap—a mile and five-eighths—worth
$37,180 to the winner.

The Black stood quietly in the Number 3 stall while
the remaining horses entered the gate and crewmen
scrambled busily about the framework.

Alec noted that the flags on the infield pole were
barely moving, so the brisk wind that had accompanied

the earlier rain had died and would be no factor in the race. The track, however, was deep and cuppy. In the great stands, some eighty thousand people, all wrought to a high pitch of excitement, awaited the starting bell.

Adjusting his goggles, Alec looked down the long homestretch, for they were starting the race on the final bend of the far turn. It would look a lot longer the next time around, when the Black would feel most his heavy impost of 141 pounds. In many respects, this might well be their toughest race of the year, against a field of four top handicap horses, all lightly weighted. With Pam watching, Alec hoped he could stay out of trouble. He wanted to race his best for her.

Alec glanced at the golden chestnut in the Number 2 stall on his left. Sun Dancer was the second favorite and startlingly big, over seventeen hands, as tall as the Black. Every part of him was in proper proportion: neck, body and legs all finely balanced, head held high, arrogant and handsome. He was eager to go; his foreleg struck the grilled door and it opened as it was designed to do, being a safety precaution. A crewman quickly closed it again.

Astride Sun Dancer was young Mario Santos, whose popularity with New York fans was greater than ever since Alec had watched him and Becky Moore race to the wire together. Mario continued to ride more winners at Aqueduct than any other jockey, and the fans had made him and his mount second favorite to the Black.

On Sun Dancer's left, in the Number 1 stall, was

his stablemate, Brush Fire. Both horses had been entered by Aqueduct's leading trainer, Mel Miller. Like Mario Santos, Miller was a favorite son of New York fans for he seldom raced his horses elsewhere. Also, he had skill, energy and youth, and was using them all to his advantage. He was willing to gamble on new, young riders and he had put Becky Moore up on Brush Fire.

Brush Fire, a blood bay with long black mane and tail, was going very light. Few male riders could have ridden at 101 pounds and, while Brush Fire was considered only a sprinter, he would be a serious threat at that weight. He was a small horse, his body short and close coupled, his every movement one of marvelous control. He made Sun Dancer, next to him, appear even bigger than he actually was.

Alec looked at Becky's face, so young and inexperienced compared with the men's. How many more races before she looked like them? How much resilience was there in her lean, feminine body? Again, Becky was meeting Mario face to face, but this time they were riding for the same stable.

Displaying his first signs of impatience, the Black tossed his head and shifted his feet nervously within the close confines of the stall. Alec spoke to him, aware that the other horses, too, were moving about, all impatient for the race to begin. There was a shimmering of colored silks in the sun.

On his right, in Number 4 stall, was Grey Mist— a tall, leggy horse, awkward when getting away but cap-

able of great speed and going a long distance, two miles
if necessary, when his strides smoothed out. But now he
was a hot, nervous and anxious horse, throwing himself
from one side of his stall to the other, and holding up
the start.

Carrying only 115 pounds, Grey Mist had the aged
veteran, Mike Costello, on his back. Alec recalled that
it was Mike who had befriended Becky in the last race
he'd seen at Aqueduct. That would not be necessary today.

Grey Mist reared and Mike used all his strength
to bring him down. But it was of no use, and there was
the danger of Grey Mist's taking a back flip. Mike
grabbed the sides of the stall and got clear of him while a
crewman scrambled over the gate's framework to grab
the horse's head. After a brief struggle, he brought him
down. Slowly, carefully, Mike eased himself back into
the saddle, but his round, wrinkled face was drained of
all color.

Alec knew that Mike, as a young man, had ridden
against Henry, and they were close friends. Although
Mike had become one of the great jockeys of all time, and
still loved to race, it was time that he quit for good, Alec
decided. Mike had retired in the past, only to come back.
Now he looked unhappy as well as scared. He'd had very
few winners this year, and this race didn't seem promising for him.

The official starter in his high perch beside the gate
called, "Mike, you okay?"

" 'Tis grateful I am to you for askin'," the jockey answered in his Irish brogue. "If I do say so meself, a horse the likes of him is not easy on an old mon."

Alec smiled grimly at Mike's determined good humor. The old jockey's body was thin as an iron rail, but it was also just as hard. Only his many years of experience had enabled him to get clear of 1200 pounds of rearing, plunging horse a moment ago. If he had been a little slower sliding off, Mike would have been under those hoofs instead of where he was sitting now. Mike sounded cocky but he wasn't, no more than the rest of them. Racing was a hard way to make what a lot of people considered an easy living.

The Black snorted at all the commotion and then he, too, went up in the air. Alec brought him down, but it was no less work for him than it had been for Mike.

In the outside stall, Sailor, a rangy bay horse, carrying 115 pounds, fussed a bit and then became quiet. Sailor had a good record, always being a contender in any race over a mile. But Alec was more fearful of Sailor's jockey, Pete Edge, than he was of the horse. Pete could rate a horse better than any other jockey in the country.

Sailor was the third choice in the race, and Pete, more than the horse, was responsible for it. Pete was a fighter on and off the track, and everybody stayed clear of him. He was built square and very strong. His left eyelid drooped slightly and a long scar ran directly beneath it, the result of a bad spill under steel-shod hoofs. It made him look extra tough, which he was. Pete had won more races in which he was thought to have had no chance than any other jockey in the country.

Alec saw him shake up his horse by kicking him in the belly. Sailor was too still for the break to come and Pete, obviously, didn't want him to fall asleep. They might be slow getting away, Alec decided, but he'd find them close by when they passed this spot again.

Brush Fire broke through the door of his Number 1 stall, and the red-coated outrider headed him off and caught him before he'd gone very far from the gate. Alec watched them come back, with Becky looking very sheepish at the catcalls coming from the stands. Wearing protective helmet and goggles, she would never have been taken for a girl. There was nothing feminine about her now.

The waiting horses shifted their feet nervously, some of them already running their races in the gate.

"Don't move," Alec told the Black. "Let the others fuss, but you settle down like the good campaigner you are." He felt the heavy strips of lead beneath his knees. They were forward on the withers where they were supposed to be. The pad was buckled down tight. It would not slip forward or backward or from side to side. It would stay there while the Black was in full flight.

The starter was having a difficult time getting them off, for now Sun Dancer had twisted in his stall and Mario Santos was kicking him, trying to straighten him out, but he only made matters worse.

"You don't punch horses around," Alec thought.

"They can get mad in a hurry and show a jock how small he is."

Mario's dark skin was stretched drum-tight across his high cheekbones, making his eyes seem all the more sunken and piercing. He looked furious and ravaged and hungry. The lean, poverty-stricken years in Puerto Rico had left their mark on him. Racing success meant a great deal to Mario, and Sun Dancer was the best horse he had been engaged to ride. He didn't mean to let such an opportunity slip by.

Sun Dancer flayed the sides of his padded stall and a crewman scrambled across the framework to assist Mario.

Alec knew that Mel Miller's strategy was to use both Brush Fire and Sun Dancer to defeat the Black. It was common knowledge that Miller had entered Brush Fire with his brilliant early speed as a "rabbit" to set a furious pace for the Black to follow; then Sun Dancer with his great staying power would come on in the homestretch, trying to finish the job of beating the champion.

Two against one. Alec was not fearful of such race strategy. He would decide what to do when he saw what kind of a pace Brush Fire set.

Alec took one final glance at Brush Fire, who didn't seem to be bothered by the wild antics of his stablemate. He was quiet but up against the bit, looking fresh and full of run. He wore red blinkers and his head sat well on a short, muscular neck.

Alec believed Becky would try to win with him, despite the fact that he was being used as a sacrificial

128

"rabbit" to Sun Dancer. This was her big opportunity as well as Mario's. She'd hang on as long as she could.

Sun Dancer had been straightened out in his stall. They were all ready to go now and waiting. High-pitched cries of the jockeys to the starter continued to shatter the air, but they meant nothing. The starter was about to push the button that opened the electrically operated doors. Just beyond, an assistant starter held a red flag in the air, ready to drop it at the sound of the starting bell.

The Black was full of fire and Alec could hardly hold him. He hoped it would be a clean start, a truly run race; that was all he asked.

The grilled doors clanged open, the starting bell rang, and the red flag came down. The Manhattan Handicap was on!

17 • *The Manhattan Handicap*

The Black and Grey Mist broke together, with Mike Costello using his whip in an attempt to get the lead. The plunging bodies of the two horses brushed slightly but it was of no consequence. Alec urged the Black on, determined to get in the clear.

Sun Dancer, surprisingly, had been first off at the break and was a length in front, followed closely by Brush Fire, who had his red-hooded head stretched out while Becky Moore rocked in the saddle as if determined to achieve her rightful place as pace-setter.

The crowd, watching the start, roared its approval of

this unpredicted early sprinting duel between stable-mates.

Alec decided quickly not to push the Black until they had straightened out from the turn and begun the run down the homestretch for the first time. There was plenty of distance to go, plenty of time. He allowed Mike Costello to take Grey Mist past him. Out of the corner of his eye he saw Sailor on the far outside and behind, a good two lengths late in getting out of the gate, as expected.

Sun Dancer maintained his jump on Brush Fire. Mario Santos seemed determined to stay in front regardless of what the pre-race strategy might have been. Becky continued to ride Brush Fire in an all-out drive, attempting to take the lead from Mario.

Alec wondered if the race had turned out to be a face-to-face duel between the two riders despite their trainer's instructions. Some young riders were stubborn and rode races as they saw them, rather than as planned. He'd done it many times himself, doing things Henry had told him *not* to do. Lots of unforeseen things happened in a race that couldn't be explained by anybody.

As they raced past the stands, the eyes of the crowd were on the blinding speed duel in progress between Sun Dancer and Brush Fire. Grey Mist raced a length behind, followed by the Black and Sailor.

The Black had settled into stride and Alec was content to wait until the right time to make his move. Meanwhile, he was saving ground, just off the rail and directly behind Sun Dancer. Grey Mist was racing on his right, a half-length ahead, a little too close, with his hindquarters only four or five inches away, not bothering the Black but vital if anything happened.

The voices of the huge crowd rose in an ever-mounting crescendo, then without warning their cheers turned to gasps and screams of alarm. *Sun Dancer had stumbled!*

The chestnut horse recovered, but Mario Santos, who had been rocking wildly in the saddle, lost his balance and was flipped over his mount's head. He hit the ground and lay in a sprawling heap before the oncoming field.

Alec shortened rein when Sun Dancer stumbled. He saw Mario fall to the ground directly in the Black's path. Then he heard the thud of the Black's hoofs against Mario's helmet, as his horse jumped over the stricken rider. A sickening tautness came to Alec's stomach, but he had no choice but to go on.

He took up the Black sharply to avoid colliding with the riderless Sun Dancer. Brush Fire, on the inside, was checked by Becky, then regained his strides quickly. Grey Mist, who had raced clear of the accident, was now in the lead.

Alec let out the wet leather in his hands. He drove the Black clear of the free-running Sun Dancer. Accidents were part and parcel of his trade. He must not think of Mario now.

Brush Fire caught Grey Mist. They raced head and head, fighting for the lead. Alec decided to go after them rather than wait any longer.

As Alec made his move, the riderless Sun Dancer

veered toward him, blocking his way. Once more Alec had to check the Black. His horse pushed hard against the bit, not taking kindly to the restraining hold Alec had on him. On his right, Sailor raced with Pete Edge, making up as much ground as he could. The big horse was now running in smooth, gigantic strides.

Reaching the center of the track, Alec found Sun Dancer still on his left and Sailor on his right. They raced in close quarters to the pounding beat of hoofs. Sun Dancer began drifting out more in front of him. It was tight, too tight, Alec decided quickly. If he stayed where he was or tried to bull his way through the two horses, there'd be trouble. As it was, he could easily clip one of their heels.

The Black shook his head furiously as Alec checked him again. Angered and frustrated by the prolonged restraint, the Black suddenly bolted out of control. He twisted his head and body to free himself of rein and bit and hands. Then he plunged between the two hard-running horses before him.

Alec could not stop him from bumping Sailor hard, almost upsetting him. Pete Edge shouted angrily, while seeking to steady his horse, but Alec was already away, the Black racing forward with a tremendous burst of speed that swept him clear of both horses. Still out of control, the Black took a direct path for the clubhouse turn. Within seconds he had moved in sharply on Grey Mist, who was matching strides with Brush Fire on the rail.

Alec saw Mike Costello glance his way, a startled look of warning on his face. Despite all Alec could do, the Black moved over against Grey Mist, forcing him into Brush Fire along the inside.

Mike Costello pulled up Grey Mist, steadying him, helping him to regain his balance, and then came on again. Becky Moore, to avoid going into the rail, had to check Brush Fire severely, and fell far behind.

Rounding the clubhouse turn, the Black threw on full power. Now he was in headlong flight, his nose stretched out and nostrils wide, as if enjoying his hard-won freedom.

Coming off the turn and into the backstretch, Alec took up the reins, shortening them again. The Black responded, his strides slowing obediently, as if he had proved his point and no longer wished to challenge his rider's authority.

Alec glanced back. Grey Mist remained in contention several lengths behind, but Brush Fire hadn't recovered from the jostling on the turn and was well out of the race. Sailor was the closest of all, a length back. The riderless Sun Dancer, who had caused all the trouble, was coming to a stop.

No two races were ever alike, Alec thought, and this was the worst he had experienced. Despite the fact that the Black was out in front and well on his way to crossing the line first, Alec knew they were far from winning it officially. Too many horses had been impeded from running their race. There had been too much body contact, too much interference and, unfortunately, he and the Black were responsible for most of it. The jockeys would lodge their claims of interference as soon as the race was over and before the results became official.

Going into the far turn, Pete Edge drove Sailor up to the Black's hindquarters. But Alec gave the Black another notch in the reins and the champion drew away to win with complete authority. For the first time in Alec's riding career, he heard catcalls and boos mingled with cheers as he rode his horse under the wire.

Later, when he came back to the finish, the Black was not taken into the winner's circle. The riders had made their claims of interference, as Alec had expected. Pete Edge claimed that the Black had bumped his mount in the first stretch, almost upsetting him. Becky Moore claimed that her horse had been forced into the rail by Grey Mist and had not recovered. And Mike Costello claimed that the Black had forced him into Becky's mount. Such objections were not rare in racing but this was the first time they had been made against the champion and Alec Ramsay.

While Alec waited with the other riders for the track stewards to examine the pictures taken by the film patrol, he learned that Mario Santos had walked to the ambulance after the accident, apparently unhurt except for a broken right arm. Alec's relief was so great that whatever decision the stewards made as to the official order of finish was secondary.

Five minutes later the order of finish was given and

the race became official. The Black was disqualified and placed fourth. Sailor was named the winner. Brush Fire was moved up to second, and Grey Mist remained third.

The Black's running time on the electric board was a new stakes record by four-fifths of a second, but the disqualification seriously marred the glossy record of the champion. As far as the stewards were concerned, Alec was the culprit. They suspended him from racing for ten days.

18 ◆ *Wall of Silence*

When they reached the stable area, the press and cameramen were waiting for them. Henry was uncooperative. If he answered their questions at all it was in terse statements.

Alec bore the brunt of much of the old trainer's criticism and impatience. "If you'd been quicker thinking," he muttered to Alec, "it wouldn't have happened. Too slow. Your mind was on other things."

Alec said nothing, knowing Henry was in one of his worst moods. He held the Black on a lead shank while the stallion was washed, his heated body steaming like damp fire.

"Deb, get a move on," Henry shouted at the groom. "Don't stand there gawking into the cameras. Give me that sponge. I'll wash him myself."

Henry squeezed the sponge over the Black's head and the water ran down, carrying sweat with it. The Black shook his head and reared, scattering the crowd.

"Keep him down, Alec!" Henry roared. "Put that chain over his nose."

Alec ignored Henry's order while the Black pawed the ground and snorted with impatience. All eyes were on him. They saw his strength and beauty even in defeat. He did not know that victory had been snatched from him.

"Mario was lucky," a columnist said. "He got off with a busted arm."

"His helmet saved him from more serious injury," another added. "The Black clipped him good."

"Yeah he's lucky, but he won't be riding in the Empire State Handicap next Saturday . . . no more than Alec will."

Henry continued washing the Black and paid no attention to the newsmen. His hands swept the stallion's glistening body in long strokes along the back, neck, sides and rump. He worked fast, splashing water intentionally over everybody.

The photographers stepped back, covering the lens of their cameras. One said chidingly, well aware of Henry's attitude toward girl jockeys and annoyed by the old trainer's tactics, "The scoop has it that Mel Miller's thinking of putting Becky Moore up on Sun Dancer next Satur-

138

day. She might win it all. How does that sit with you, Henry? I mean, a girl winning a $100,000 handicap which could have been yours."

Henry continued his work, ignoring that question as he had the others. He changed water often, barking orders when Deb didn't have the pails ready fast enough for him or when Alec allowed the Black too much freedom. Finally, he put the stallion's long tail in a pail and sloshed it around in the water, then whisked it in the air, once more splashing the faces, the clothes, the cameras of the newsmen. They stepped back again, not liking it and resenting Henry's hostile, uncooperative attitude.

Alec didn't blame them. Henry was taking the Black's disqualification as a personal affront. Or was it that of all the trainers at Aqueduct Henry disliked Mel Miller the most and the suggestion that Miller might win the $100,-000 race with a girl rider was more than Henry could bear, especially at this moment of defeat.

Alec looked down the shed row where Miller's victory party was already in progress. While the popular trainer had not won first money, he'd pocketed well over $12,000 for Brush Fire's second place. Even more reason for celebration was that he'd beaten the Black, officially if not by having the faster horse.

The caterer's truck had just arrived and there was enough champagne and food for everyone in the area. Miller did not restrict his parties to his stable alone. *All* caretakers, riders and trainers in the area were invited. He endeared himself to everyone, including the press;

in fact, he was as popular with them as with horsemen. He was affable, courteous and cooperative, remaining calm when besieged by newsmen and doing his best to fulfill their requests. He was, Alec admitted, a far different person from Henry.

The Black's dripping body had the ripple of fine silk as Henry removed most of the water with long sweeps of the curved scraper. The splendid play of his muscles was evidence of the skillful care and training given him, and Henry, despite his shortcomings, had played an important part in bringing the Black to his finest shape. No one could be perfect, Alec decided. Everyone had to take the bad with the good. Each had to live with another's faults as well as his own. The most important thing was to have respect for the other person. He thought of Pam, for she would have said something like that. He wondered if she was on her way to the stable area. She had promised to see him after the race, but her visit wasn't going to make things any easier. It wasn't as he'd planned at all.

Alec saw Mel Miller leave the party and walk toward them. It was not something Alec had expected or cared to see. Miller, with all his courtesy, was blunt, even brazen, in his conversations with Henry. He'd told him in no uncertain terms that he could beat the Black if the weights were right. Worse still in Henry's eyes, Miller had been the first trainer in the New York area to break the sex bar, boosting Becky Moore into the saddle six months ago.

Now he strode toward them, slim, too tall ever to
have been a jockey, handsome and very confident. He
looked like a young man very much in charge of the responsibilities to which he had set his hand. And well he
should, Alec decided, for he had been very successful
patching up sick horses, after buying them cheap, and
making winners out of them. He had come a long way in
just a few years of training, and now had an active public
stable, thanks to his zeal and skill.

Miller ignored Henry and directed his invitation to
the newsmen. "Come on over, boys," he said good-na-
turedly, "the party's on."

The newsmen were well aware of the friction between
the two trainers and, in their own interests, they en-
couraged it now.

"Is it true you're putting Becky Moore up on Sun Dancer Saturday?" a reporter asked.

"Sure. I like the way she rides, and she's the best in-
vestment I have after Mario." He glanced at the Black,
then added jovially, "We'll win it."

"You mean with the Black out of the race you don't
expect any trouble?" the reporter asked.

"That's what I mean, but even if he was in, he's not
unbeatable. Like today," Miller added quietly.

Henry remained silent. Finished with the scraper, he
used a clean sponge and, squeezing it dry, went all over
the Black again.

"Too many trainers believe what you fellows are writing about the Black," Miller said wisely. "I'm not one

of them. I don't scare easily. Something can always happen to the big horse. Or maybe Alec here is losing what he had for so long. Good racing calls for good riding. A little bit of luck can have a big bearing on what happens. Give me an inch and I'll take a mile. Give me a chance at the purse and I'll make it a horse race."

The newsmen were enjoying the remarks of this cocky young man. Once again he was writing their stories for them.

"Did Sun Dancer come out of his gallop okay?" one of the reporters asked.

"Absolutely. Not a scratch on him. If he hadn't stumbled . . ." Miller looked at Henry but the old trainer had his back to him. He went on, ". . . . well, the weights were right today and I'd been holding Sun Dancer in reserve for this race. It would have been a horse race."

Henry finished his work and said quietly, "Walk him, Alec. Better if you do it than Deb. Cool him out carefully, now. Just a few swallows of water slowly, and warm it up some . . . don't want it cold. Off with him now."

Without a word to anyone else, Henry turned abruptly and went to the tack room, closing the door behind him.

After walking the Black dry, Alec took him to his stall. He ran a hand down the stallion's left foreleg and found it cold to the touch as it should have been. Lifting the leg he looked at the foot. There was a wafer-thin piece of leather beneath the shoe that kept the dirt and sand from working its way into a sore spot which had given him trouble in the past.

The Black could use a rest, if only for a short while, and now that they had Black Sand in the stable, Alec decided to ask Henry to send the champion home for a while, to give him a change of scene, if nothing else. He had been tight today, too tight, and much too difficult to handle.

Taking a pair of small tongs from his pocket, Alec went over the raised foot, closing the jaws of the instrument on different parts. The Black never flinched. There was no sign of sensitivity or anything wrong.

"His feet are cleaner than mine," a voice said from the doorway.

Alec turned so quickly that he lost his balance and sat in the straw. "Hey," he said, realizing Pam must have been watching him for a long time. Her head rested comfortably on her arms as she leaned over the half-door.

Before he could warn her not to come inside, she'd opened the door and the Black had gone forward, his head bent and neck arched. Fearful that he would bite her, Alec jumped to his feet and went after him.

He saw immediately that he had nothing to fear. Even the Black seemed to sense Pam's trust and love of all animals. As if to honor her trust, he strutted for her, dancing on all four legs and waving his mane in the air, displaying all the delicacy of his marvelous balance. Finally, he stood still, very collected and proud, his great eyes flashing.

143

"Oh, Alec," she said in quiet awe, "he's so handsome, more handsome than I ever dreamed. Just as you said, you have to be this close to him to *know*." She tossed her hair back. "I know it isn't for his beauty and pretty ways that you love him, Alec, but see the crimson flower in his eyes!"

Alec moved to her side to find out what she meant. With Pam here, he thought, he must be prepared to see many new things. The Black's eyes were shining with a red glow that had terrified many people in the past. Pam saw it as a crimson flower.

"It didn't work out very well today," Alec said. "You chose the wrong day to come. I'm sorry."

"You couldn't help what happened."

"But it happened anyway. I've been set down for ten days."

"You mean you can't ride?"

"Not in a race."

"You can use the rest," she said, laughing. "You look lots more tired than he does."

"I rode Black Sand for Henry this morning," he said, wanting to change the subject from himself.

"Did he like him?"

"Very much. But the colt didn't go for me like he does for you. He's used to you."

"Does Henry know I'm here?"

"I told him you were taking the day off to watch the race. He didn't expect you to come backside."

"Why not?"

144

Alec shrugged his shoulders. "He figured you'd be too scared of him, I guess."

"That's crazy. I'm not scared of anybody."

"Henry doesn't know that," Alec said. "Did you see the colt?"

"Yes, I stopped there first. He looks happy."

"Not as happy as he'd be at the farm, maybe, but he's adjusting."

"I think he likes all the activity," she said, looking outside at the crowd gathered around Mel Miller's stable. "That's a wild party going on over there."

A slim figure in blue jeans and a blue work shirt walked past, followed closely by a huge dog.

"That's Becky Moore," Alec said, "the girl who rode Brush Fire."

"Who's her companion?"

"I don't know his name. I never got close enough to him to find out. He's her bodyguard, sleeps with one eye open, they say, for protection."

"I wouldn't think she'd need it."

"That's catty," Alec said.

"I didn't mean it that way. I meant that she looks like she can take care of herself."

"She should," Alec admitted. "She's been around a long time, but always with her dog."

"So she trusts nobody."

"Nobody."

Alec and Pam left the Black's stall and walked toward the closed tack room. "You're sure you want to meet

145

Henry now?" he asked.

"Why not?" she said, laughing. "I'm crazy enough to trust *everybody*."

"He's not in one of his best moods."

"That's okay," she said.

Reaching the tack room, Alec opened the door and found Henry sitting in the chair, his face brooding, an unread newspaper on his lap.

"Henry," he said, entering the room. "I want you to meet Pam."

19 ◆ *A Bag of Beliefs*

Henry rose to his feet in deference to Pam's femininity, but there was nothing courteous in his voice or manner when he said to Alec, "I thought I told you not to bring her around here."

"I thought you might change your mind when you met her," Alec answered.

"Wow," Pam said good-humoredly, "we're off to a great beginning."

Henry pushed his body against the back wall of the room, his hands on his vast hips, his lower lip drooped in a grim smile. He looked at Pam in complete silence, examining her, taking his time.

Henry's first impressions confirmed what he had expected, a very pretty girl. Her long, thick blond hair waved and floated below her shoulders. She wore a yellow blouse and short skirt, her legs bare and slender. She had a very delicate oval face with piercing eyes of a remarkable blue.

"Well, it can't be helped now," he said resignedly. "And since you're here I'd like to thank you for the good job you've done for us, especially with Black Sand." He paused as if waiting for her to acknowledge his compliment, his gratitude.

Pam obliged. "It was more fun than work," she said.

"Well, whatever it was," Henry said, "I'm afraid we must let you go. I've found a man who's exactly right for the job, one we've been trying to get for a long time. It's Mike Costello, Alec," he explained, turning to the boy. "You know Mike's always said he'd never retire while he was winning races. Well he hasn't been doing that this season as you know. So he's decided to turn in his silks and work for us. He'll do a great job at the farm."

Alec's face had whitened beneath his tan. "No," he said. "We need Pam too."

Henry shook his head. "You know as well as I do that we don't need *two* people working colts."

"Then why did you tell me Pam could stay?" Alec asked angrily.

"That was before I knew Mike was available," Henry answered. "But listen," he went on kindly. "I know what

148

this girl means to you and I'm willing to go along. Maybe we can find something else for her to do at the farm."

"No," Pam said, interrupting them. "It's time I moved on anyway."

Alec turned to her. "I'm not letting you go, Pam."

"It'll make things easier," she said, her eyes looking for understanding. "Besides Henry is right. From the very first, it went with the job. *Temporary* until you found professional help. Remember?"

"That's all been changed," Alec said.

Pam put her hand on his. "It's not *over*," she said. "Stop thinking that it is. I just don't want to copy your world, Alec, or anyone else's. I've got my own. So please . . ."

Henry was surprised that Pam had agreed to leave without an argument. Then he remembered that she was a drifter like so many young people today, hypnotized by loud music and fantastic, unfulfillable dreams. He was afraid of the effect she might already have had on Alec, that Alec might even become like her.

In defense of Alec's goals as well as his own, Henry said, "The trouble with *your* world, young lady, is that it holds a promise that can't be fulfilled, that of a paradise here on earth. I feel sorry for you and those like you."

Alec said angrily, "Cut it out, Henry. That kind of talk has no place here."

"Maybe it does," Pam said, turning to the trainer. "Don't you too dream of such a world?" she asked Henry.

Henry smiled but his eyes belied any friendliness, "If

I did, I wouldn't be very realistic," he said.

"Who can say where reality begins and ends?" she asked.

"Listen," Henry said, "everyone is searching for a better way of life, including me. But you'll learn you can't change human nature." His attitude, like his voice, was severe and authoritative.

Pam shrugged her shoulders. "Maybe so," she said. "But did you ever think, Henry, that maybe it's not human nature that won't change but *us?* I mean, we all know what's important in life but most of us won't live it."

"That's ridiculous," Henry said. "You're walking on clouds. Why don't you admit that you just don't want to be fenced in? That you're one of those 'freedom' kids who has no respect for dedication and duty?"

"*Dedication and duty,*" she repeated. "To whom, Henry? Or to what?"

"To one's job. One's life," Henry answered. He returned to his chair and picked up the newspaper, apparently ending the meeting.

But Pam wasn't finished. "We're not running scared like you think, Henry," she said, angry for the first time. "We're only turning off what you believe is so great. Who said we have to make it by your standards? Or have the same goals you do? That doesn't mean you can't do your thing too, if it makes you happy. *But leave us alone.*"

Alec said bitterly, "Come on, Pam. I told you it wouldn't work out." He opened the door.

Henry stared at the boy's back, knowing Alec was furious. "Wait a minute," he said, putting down the paper. "I don't want to end our visit this way. It's not going to do any of us any good." He paused, looking at them steadily.

"Maybe you've got something, Pam," he conceded finally. "Maybe I'm just too old to see it, that's all. I'd like to be friends. Will you accept me as I am?"

"Sure," she said quickly, "if you'll accept me as *I* am. But no more labels. Okay?"

"What does that mean?"

"Pinning labels on kids so you'll know what we stand for, then filing us away."

"Okay," Henry said. "I'll try."

Alec stood beside the door, undecided whether to leave or not. He wasn't certain that Henry wasn't playing some kind of a game. If Henry wanted to be friends with Pam, he was doing it for his own reasons. Henry had rules but they were those he made up himself.

"Let's be honest," the trainer told Pam. "You're not just another troubled kid or you couldn't have done such a good job at the farm. You're a horseman. That's why I'm talking to you."

Pam's face stiffened. "Nobody's just *another troubled kid,*" she said, her words coming quick and keen.

Alec knew the old man was infuriated by Pam's outspoken reprimand, even though he didn't let it show. Henry was used to unquestioned obedience from people as well as horses.

151

Henry sighed and said patiently, "Okay, I'll remember not to put it that way again. Don't get your back up."

"My back's not up," Pam said quietly.

Henry was playing it cool, Alec decided, but so was Pam. For what reason? What did Henry have to gain by it?

"Anyway," Henry went on, "I didn't ask you to stay to discuss your generation. I've got a problem that's a bit larger than that. Maybe you can help me with it."

"I can help *you?*" Pam asked, truly surprised.

Alec too was taken off guard by Henry's request for assistance. He turned to Pam, hoping she wouldn't be caught unprepared by Henry's solicitude. The bare light bulb above her head cast a severe, searching brightness on her face. It showed the high, sharp cheekbones, the long-lashed eyes, the very tanned skin.

Alec was disturbed that the wariness he had seen earlier in Pam's face was gone. It had been replaced by trust. "Careful, Pam," he wanted to warn. But Henry's next remark was directed at him, and it was he who was caught unprepared, not Pam.

"Alec and I are at dagger points you might say," the trainer said. "He's breaking rules we've lived by for years."

Pam stared at Henry with ever-widening eyes, then she turned to Alec. "Did you hear that?"

"I heard," Alec said. "I guess it's true—the dagger points anyway. But I don't know what rules I've been breaking. What are they, Henry?"

"Very funny," Henry answered. "Maybe Mel Miller said it better a while ago. Remember? '. . . *Alec is losing what he had for so long. Good racing calls for good riding.*'"

"I didn't think you heard him," Alec said. "You weren't paying much attention to him or the reporters."

"*I heard,*" Henry said. "*And I agree.*"

Alec's shirt was sticking to his body with a damp, clammy feeling. "That's something," he said with attempted lightness. "You *agreeing* with Miller." The whole thing was getting even more ridiculous. Here they were arguing again, and this time in front of Pam.

"Don't be sarcastic," Henry said. "I'm only trying to help. You've got your mind on too many other things to race properly."

Pam said, "Alec has every right to be his own kind of person, not what you think he should be."

Henry snorted and turned to her. "There you go again with your *ideals,*" he said in a great burst of rage. "You kids can make this the kind of world you want after I'm gone. I'm concerned with the world Alec's facing every time he gets up on a horse and has to contend with men who are as eager to win as he is.

"It's no pretty-colored world out there. It can kill. I mean dead, not maimed or injured. What happened to Mario Santos today was an example. A few more inches and he would have had it. It could happen tomorrow or the next day to Alec, the way he's riding. What am I going to do about that?"

153

Alec left the door to return to Pam's side. "You're being over-dramatic, Henry," he said.

"Oh I am, am I?" The trainer glared at Alec. "What were you thinking of today when Mario and Becky beat you at the start? Was it Pam? Girl riders? Or what?"

"It was neither," Alec said. "They broke faster than we did, that's all." But in fairness to Henry, he recalled another race when he'd been thinking of Pam and got away late.

"It cost you the race," Henry said. "If you'd come out first, you would have avoided the accident."

"You can't blame Alec for a horse stumbling in front of him," Pam said.

Henry turned to her. "No, I can't," he said. "I blame him only for being in a bad position, when he could have avoided it. Even a girl might have done better."

"Any girl?" she asked.

Henry studied Pam, wondering if she meant what he thought she did. "Even *you*," he said finally.

"I didn't mean me," she said. "I just wondered why you use girls' riding to mean poor riding. Does good riding mean *men only?*"

"It does in racing," Henry said. "Girls don't belong in it."

"That's crazy," Pam said, "if that's what they want to do. Even I've raced some, and against men too."

"Where?"

"Fairs and 'brush' races in Virginia mostly."

Henry chuckled. "That's another world, not the one

154

I'm talking about." He paused, studying her face a long while before turning to Alec.

"How would you like her to find out what it's all about, Alec?" he challenged. "Maybe that would help settle a lot of things between us. What if I let her start Black Sand? You said the colt goes better for her than he does for you."

Alec was astounded by Henry's abrupt challenge. He knew the trainer was daring him as well as Pam to face up to what Henry considered the realities of racing.

"We'd pick an easy race, a cheap one," Henry continued. "Nothing but a schooling race, really. She'd be doing nothing more than what she's been doing at the farm except in the company of others. How does that sound to you?"

No race was ever an easy race, Alec knew, and he was concerned for Pam's safety. Yet she could ride with the best of them and, if she raced, it might mean that she wouldn't leave. "It's up to Pam," he said, turning to her.

"Well, Pam?" Henry asked. His words meant something more to each of them. *Put up or shut up about girls having a place in racing,* he might have said.

Alec had only to look at Pam's face to know what her answer would be. Regardless of how she felt about big-time racing, the thrill of riding her colt in his first competition and responding to Henry's dare were overwhelming.

"Sure," she said. "Why not?"

155

20 · *The Drummers*

The following Wednesday afternoon, Pam went to the post with Black Sand—the first race on the program, the first race for each of them. Alec watched her with mixed emotions and some misgivings, now that the moment of trial was at hand. But he wanted Pam to remain with him, and the thrill of racing Black Sand might be the incentive she needed.

Henry had wasted no time, once Pam had agreed to ride. The morning following their meeting he'd had Pam work Black Sand, arranging for a track steward to be there. They had watched Pam break the colt from the gate in the company of two other horses and male riders, a six furlong test of Pam's competence as a jockey to obtain her apprentice's license. She had gone the distance in a good 1:14, beating one rival by five lengths and outdistancing the other.

Alec had heard the steward tell Henry, "She'll have no trouble. She has a fine pair of hands and knows what she's doing."

Henry too had been impressed by Pam's performance. Later, back at the barn, he'd asked Alec, "Where did she learn to ride like that?" And Alec had told him of the professional horsemen in Pam's life who, she'd said, had taught her everything she knew.

"Not everything," Henry had replied. "She's naturally good. Yes, I like the way she rides."

Alec wondered if Henry was getting to like Pam personally as much as he liked her riding. There was no doubt that Pam was reaching him by her cheerfulness. For instance, she had gone to the farm on Monday to work the colts and had returned with a large bunch of wild flowers which she'd given to Henry. Alec had thought the trainer would explode with derision at her offering. Instead Henry had looked bewildered but not displeased.

"I picked them just for you," she had told him.

Alec watched the horses through his binoculars. He had found a place on the rail near the finish line, where he wanted to be when the race ended. The horses were in

157

the chute on the far side of the track. It was a large field of two-year-old colts and fillies, all non-winners. Actually, the race was a cheap one—a six-furlong race against cheap horses, the kind Henry had wanted for their colt's first start. Except for not being race-hardened, Black Sand outclassed them all.

"If Pam only stays clear of the others and rides as I told her," he thought, "she'll win easy." Fortunately, she had the outside post position in the milling field of twelve horses.

Alec moved his binoculars along the line, passing from one jockey to another. The horses would do the running but what about the hands that guided them? Each rider had professional poise and confidence. Becky Moore was there too, riding the first of her three mounts for the afternoon. She looked as confident as any of the men.

Henry couldn't have known Becky would be in the race, but the unusual coincidence was appreciated by the crowd since it added interest to an otherwise unpredictable race among erratic two-year-olds. Never before had there been two girl jockeys in the same race at Aqueduct.

"Keep clear, Pam, just keep clear," he thought, wondering if she would remember all he'd told her over and over again these past two days. She had listened intently to him but her eyes had said, *"Talk all you like, but I must do it my way when the time comes."* And he knew she was right, for experience is the only teacher.

Now, as he watched her in the black-checkered silks

of Hopeful Farm, he nervously wiped the back of his hand across his dry lips. There was nothing he could do to help her. "Okay," he said aloud, as if she could hear him. "Do it your way then. Just don't get hurt."

The starting bell rang and the grilled doors slammed open. He saw Pam slacken rein, loosen her knees and hurl the colt forward. Black Sand came out of the gate a half-stride ahead of the others.

For a few fleeting seconds, the other horses raced beside her, running ever faster to make up the leap Black Sand had on them. But the colt was not to be caught; he was running with tremendous speed and smoothness.

"*Go, Pam, Go!*" Alec shouted.

Midway down the backstretch, Black Sand was a full length in front of the jam-packed field. Pam kept him on the outside and made no attempt to move over to the rail. She was being very careful to avoid trouble.

They approached the turn and Alec watched her take Black Sand closer to the inside. She guided him with hands and body across the track, slowly, carefully toward the turn. The other horses came on and Black Sand was in closer quarters now. The colt didn't like it. His pace became rough.

Alec understood Black Sand's reluctance to move closer to the flaying whips of the oncoming riders. He saw Pam urge him on, not with her body alone but with the weight of her knowledge and understanding of what caused his fears. She was telling him with her hands, "No whip will touch you. No one will hurt you.

159

Just run your race, and soon we'll be clear again."

Black Sand lowered his head and dug in again to meet the challenge of the horses on his left. A bay horse wearing a bright-yellow hood tried to steal the lead as they curved into the turn. Beside the bay, on the inside, was another horse racing abreast. Both were trying to knife their way past still a third horse on the rail, who was tiring and bearing out. All three riders were making full use of their whips, Alec saw, using all the strength of their arms and shoulders. The strides of the horses lengthened under the drumming of the whips.

Pam kept Black Sand clear of them, even checking him a bit to lose more ground. Her reflexes were quick, Alec noted, and she was making split-second decisions. He knew she wanted to win but it was not as important to her as the colt's coming out of the race unscathed and free of any fear that might create greater problems later on. Black Sand seemed less afraid than he had just seconds ago, more confident in close quarters. That was to the good, Alec decided. Pam would simply keep him in stride and free of the closely crowded trio racing beside her. She would make her move again, when they came off the turn.

The horses bent around the turn, their riders whipping with either hand, scuffing and scrubbing with hands and feet, determined to get out in front for the final run down the homestretch. Becky Moore was just inside Pam, as free with her whip as the men. Too free, Alec decided; she was using it every second, leather striking hide rhythmically, switching from one hand to the other without pause in an attempt to keep her tiring mount on a steady course.

The horse with the yellow hood had surged into the lead, his jockey rocking and pushing to keep a stride ahead of the one beside him. Both horses were digging in, their hides scraping and moving over to the rail directly in front of Becky's mount.

Alec kept his binoculars on them. Becky was beaten, and must have known it. It was pointless for her to continue whipping her mount. Yet with another terrible blow, she launched her horse again. There was no place for him to go on the rail, for the two leaders left him no room. Lashed by the whip, he bore out toward Black Sand!

Alec watched Pam try to stay clear of him. Black Sand's strides became ragged as Becky drove her heels into her horse's sides while lashing him with all her strength.

For the first time during the race, Alec felt the coldness of fear. Becky would stop at nothing in her determination to keep her mount going. She had switched her whip, from left hand to right, in an attempt to straighten out her mount and drive him between horses.

Pam checked Black Sand abruptly as Becky's whip came hissing down.

Whether or not it touched Black Sand on the legs, Alec couldn't see. It might have been that the colt was just frightened by it. But, suddenly, Black Sand took two

161

quick jumps to the outside. Pam tried to stop him as he bolted crazily across the track. Alec caught a glimpse of the outer rail and knew that the colt would run full tilt into it. *"No!"* he shouted at the top of his voice.

Black Sand's hurtling body crashed into the fence and Pam was catapulted high into the air!

Alec had jumped the rail and was on the track, running for the far turn when the field of horses swept by. With the track clear, the ambulance left the infield gate. Alec flagged it down and hopped into the front seat.

A small crowd was already on the scene when they got there. Black Sand was dead, his neck twisted and broken. White-faced, Alec kneeled beside the still, silk-clad figure that was Pam. His forehead was drenched in cold sweat, his body trembling uncontrollably.

Pam's eyes were open but glazed. She tried to raise herself to an elbow but he prevented her by saying, "Lie still, Pam. You've had a bad fall." He moved aside for the ambulance attendants. They removed her helmet, and the sun shone on her hair with a violent light. Her face was grimy with tiny rivulets of blood running through the caked dirt. He felt tenderness and gratitude that she was alive. Her eyes turned in the direction of Black Sand, and Alec knew he had no choice but to tell her. There must be no subterfuge, no phoniness. That was the way she would want it.

"The colt's dead," he said, unable to control the quaver in his voice.

She did not answer and her silence alarmed him. He touched her face.

"Please, Pam. He didn't suffer. He didn't know what happened." Alec passed his hand over her forehead. Her whole face was cold.

Then, suddenly, her hands were seeking and clutching his. He lowered his face toward hers and she pushed her head into his chest, as if hollowing out a nest. "I know," she said, swallowing noisily. "You don't have to tell me."

Alec realized that Pam had known the moment the colt had died, for she and Black Sand had been one.

21 • *Pain and Tears*

That night, while Pam slept at Physicians' Hospital in Jackson Heights, close to the track, Alec took Black Sand's body to Hopeful Farm. There in the early morning, with the help of others, he buried the colt in the lower pasture where Black Sand had spent so many hours with Pam.

Alec tried not to be over sentimental about the burial. They took chances every day in this business, he reminded himself harshly, both with themselves and with their horses. There was a high mortality rate among breeding stock and foals as well as horses in training and racing. The risks were very great.

Pam had survived the bizarre accident, suffering only facial lacerations. The x-rays had disclosed no bone fractures, no serious injuries; she was being held at the hospital overnight only for observation. He must think of that and nothing else. What might have been for Black Sand was finished. He was a professional horseman. He could look at it no other way.

Yet, when the men had left with their tractor and shovels, Alec remained beside the newly turned earth, remembering the way it was between Black Sand and Pam, and the happiness he too had shared with them. Here he had spent many happy hours with the colt and Pam, aware of each sound, each touch, every passing minute.

Alec turned from the grave to a sky that was rippled with crimson from the rising sun. A horse neighed shrilly from a distant pasture, and on the first breeze of early morning he smelled the sweet, soft scent of wild flowers. He walked to the nearby woods and gathered a few of them, which he placed carefully around the new earth. Then he wept, unashamed.

The sun was flaring over the ridge when he left, and the birds were singing their morning hymn to summer —or, he wondered, was it for Black Sand?

In the late afternoon Alec arrived back at Aqueduct. He didn't expect to find Pam there, even if she had been discharged from the hospital. Nothing was worth the price she'd paid yesterday. There was no doubt in his mind that Becky had caused the tragic mishap, perhaps

165

not intentionally but by her relentless riding, her determination to beat men at their own game regardless of the consequences. A foul claim could have been lodged against her, Alec knew, but the finish of the race was of no importance to him or Henry. For them the race had ended on the far turn.

When he turned into the milling stable area, the first person he saw was Pam. She was swinging an empty pail on her way to a water faucet, looking like any other kid in blue Levis with slender legs and scuffy brown loafers with run-down heels. She had her back to him, but he couldn't mistake her blond hair, tied with a red ribbon and pulled to one side so that the back of her neck showed.

He hurried and caught up with her. She was leaning over, running water into the pail. Despite his great joy at finding her there, he said simply, "Hi."

She raised her eyes to his and straightened; then she moved into his arms and he held her close.

"You okay?" he asked finally.

"Sure. They let me go early this morning." She paused, then added, "Henry met me and asked that I take over Deb's job for a few days. That's why I'm here."

Alec followed her to the Black's stall. He wasn't surprised that Henry had asked Pam to stay. The trainer couldn't have done otherwise after the accident, knowing the work might help to get her mind off her fall and the loss of Black Sand. But he was surprised and pleased that Pam had accepted.

166

The black stallion turned in their direction as they entered the stall. Then with a happy neigh of greeting he moved quickly to the pail Pam offered him, playing in the water rather than drinking it.

"I took Black Sand to the farm," Alec said.

"I know. Henry told me." She turned away and went to the door.

He followed, knowing how she felt despite the firmness of her voice. And because he realized she would want to know, he told her where he had buried the colt and described the wild flowers he had placed on the new earth.

She turned to him, and rested her head on his shoulder. He put his arms around her, saying, "I'm sorry, Pam, so sorry it turned out this way."

The tiny earrings shone softly in the lobes of her ears. He was aware of her troubled breathing and felt more than ever that he was one with her.

Suddenly, the Black's warm breath wafted over their heads. The stallion bent his neck to touch Pam's cheek with his muzzle, his dark mane flowing over her blond hair.

Alec was surprised by the Black's display of affection, but he was not jealous to find that his horse loved Pam. He could not be selfish and possessive around her. She had won the stallion's affection in the same manner she had acquired Black Sand's love. It was her way with animals.

Pam spoke, her voice smothered and barely audible,

167

sounding against his chest as if the words came from inside his own body, and not from hers.

"Oh, Alec, I loved him so."

His arms tightened around her and he placed his head on hers. Her chest heaved with her troubled breathing, her bronze skin took on a pinkness.

"Henry was right about girls' racing," Alec said. "It's everything he said it was. It's not for you."

"But it's for Becky Moore?" she asked, turning her face up to him. "Is that the kind of riding it takes, Alec? Girls have to be ruthless to race? Is that what you mean?"

"I'm afraid so," Alec said.

With a movement as unexpected and as quick as a cat's, Pam took his arms from about her waist and stood apart from him. "I don't believe you," she said angrily. "I want to race again."

Alec was alarmed at the sudden change in her face, from feminine softness to a firmness he hadn't seen before. "Are you looking for more trouble?" he asked. "Isn't it enough that you learned first-hand how it can be out there?"

A queer smile came to her mouth. "And haven't you learned, as I have, that when you take a bad fall you get up and ride again?"

Alec looked at her a long while, knowing she was right —that she should race again as quickly as possible. It had been the same for him and other jockeys after bad falls. Otherwise, she would carry the memory of the accident with her the rest of her life, and perhaps never ride the same again.

"I want to finish what I began," she said. "Let me."

"But how can we do that with no Black Sand?" Alec asked. He hadn't wanted to mention the colt again, but she gave him no choice.

"By letting me ride *your* horse on Saturday," she answered.

"*My* horse? *The Black?*" he asked, stunned. "It's no good, Pam. It wouldn't work."

"Why not?"

"Lots of reasons."

"You can be plainer than that," she said.

"No one but me has ever been on his back. You couldn't handle him."

"Let me try him and see, Alec," she pleaded. "I'm not afraid. And if I can't ride him, I certainly won't race him."

Alec said nothing, aware that she was studying his face and finding something he could not keep from her. He did not want to let anyone else ride the Black. There were undefinable degrees to which the stallion could be handled without danger. But it went beyond that, Alec knew; *the Black was his and his alone.*

"Please, Alec," she said, "give me a chance."

Alec remained silent, thinking of many things—not only her ability to get along with horses, any horse, even the Black, but of their conversation that last night at the farm when she'd said, *"True love is giving up that which you love, if need be, when the time comes."* Her words meant something to him now.

Alec looked at her face in the half-light of the stall. Her mouth was slightly open, even her breathing seemed slower as she awaited his answer. He loved her too much to turn her down.

"If I thought you could get away with it," he said finally.

"But I think I can," she said.

Alec made one last assessment before coming to a decision. To handle the Black in a race called for strength, determination, skill and courage. She lacked only the strength but, perhaps, her will and her need to race were strong enough to compensate. If she was ready to take a chance, so was he.

"Wait here," he said. "I want to talk to Henry."

22 ◆ *Riding the Wind*

"It's incredible that you would even consider anyone else riding the Black," Henry told Alec in amazement. "Maybe one of our best jocks could get away with it but not a girl—not even *your* girl." He softened his voice. "Now I know you think you're in love with her, Alec, but even so there are limits to one's love. You can't do a crazy thing like this."

Alec shook his head. "I want her to *try* him, Henry, then we'll decide whether she races him or not."

"No, we won't," the trainer said angrily. "The Black does not belong to you alone, not in registration he doesn't. He belongs to the farm and the corporation, of which your father is head. And even to me, who has cared for him as well as you. You cannot risk throwing him away on this girl."

"I'm not worried about hurting *him*," Alec answered. "It's Pam who will be taking the risk." He looked down the shed-row and saw Pam coming toward them, even though he'd asked her to stay out of the discussion. Her face had a green tinge and her lips were the color of ash.

Henry turned to Pam when she joined them. He was astonished that she wanted to ride the Black although he understood her need to race again. He shared her tragic loss of Black Sand and had hoped to make amends for what he knew was partly his fault. But that did not mean he had to go along with anything as ridiculous as her racing the Black.

"You can't be serious, Alec," Henry said, returning to their discussion. "If you want to put another rider up on the Black, get the best. Get Pete Edge or Willy Walsh, but don't put up a *girl*. In fact, I won't have it any other way."

Alec did not reply immediately, and the silence between them became strained.

"I'm letting Pam try him," he said decisively. "The Black is my horse, regardless of how he's registered, and I want her to ride him."

Henry grunted in shock at Alec's outright defiance, and turned his face away. For a moment he resumed cleaning tack, a job he had begun earlier. Then without stopping his work he said quietly, "The Empire State Handicap is worth over $100,000, you know."

"I know how much it's worth," Alec said. He was also aware that when Henry talked about money, the trainer tended to be elaborately polite and even make concessions to others. "And if Pam can ride the Black," Alec went on, "isn't it worth taking a chance of winning it?"

"Maybe it is," Henry conceded in a muted, silky tone. "*If* she can ride him, that is. But if she can't, what then? Will you let Willy Walsh or Pete Edge ride him in her place? Will you?"

Alec made no immediate reply, and Henry waited a long moment before persisting. "Will you?"

Alec knew that Henry had two motives—one, his desire to crush such an amateurish suggestion that Pam ride the Black; and two, the possibility of winning $100,000 with a professional male rider in the saddle. Up to now Henry had thought they were out of the race altogether; he had never considered anyone but Alec riding the Black.

Henry waited impatiently, aware that Alec was in a spot. The old trainer kept his eyes wide and unblinking, a look of exaggerated innocence in them, as if he was content to leave the whole matter to Alec. He doubted that Alec would allow Pam to try the Black. For if she failed to handle him, Alec would be forced to have another professional jockey ride his horse.

"Well, Alec?" he prodded. "Make up your mind."

"Okay, Henry," Alec said finally. "We'll do it your

173

way. We'll put Pam up on him and see how it goes. If she can handle him, she'll race Saturday; if not——"

"If not," Henry interrupted curtly, "I'll select the *next* rider. You've made the decision, but I'll follow through on the rest. That's my end of it." His eyes left Alec to settle on the girl.

"You can try him now," he told Pam, surprising her as well as Alec. "Better now than waiting until tomorrow morning when there'll be a crowd around. Tack him up, Alec."

A short while later, Alec led the Black from his stall. Pam walked alongside, her eyes on the stallion who would test her ability as it had never been tried before.

The Black walked with a dancing pace, his neck arched high and his head swaying from left to right. He moved his ears and sniffed the air with great force. A faint sweat had already broken out on his flanks.

Alec brought him to a halt a short distance from the gap that led onto the track. There he stroked him and told him to be still. He knew the stallion's instincts went deeper than any language between them. The Black realized something extraordinary was about to happen because he'd been saddled and taken from his stall late in the afternoon with an empty track and stands before him. His muscles were tense, his breathing quick.

Henry's eyes remained on Pam, looking for a sign of fear, half expecting her to change her mind now that the moment had come. "A child weighs more than she does," he thought. "Where would she get the strength to handle such a horse?" He did not think she would go ahead with her ridiculous plan to ride the Black, not when she finished looking at him and could plainly see what was in store for her.

Alec kept the Black away from Pam; the stallion was moving much too restlessly to be mounted. It was only a game, Alec knew, but very dangerous if one was not alert. He was putting his horse, his pride, his heart on the line, all without knowing if Pam would be safe.

The Black feigned impatience and rebellion against the bridle. On trembling legs he pawed the ground, then half-reared, his mane waving high, his eyes flashing.

"It's getting late," Henry said. "We'd better get started if we're going to do this today." Yet he made no move toward the horse, knowing it was for Alec to decide when Pam should mount.

Pam approached the stallion. "I'm ready, whenever you are," she told Alec.

"In a minute," he answered sharply, surprised to find her beside him.

Pam began whistling the same notes she'd used to attract Black Sand's attention in the past. Alec was going to order her to stop, and then decided against it.

She will do it her way, anyway, he thought. *Leave her alone. I'm only upsetting them both by my own uneasiness.*

Pam spoke to the Black in a voice that was no less soft than her whistling. All the while she moved closer to him, well within range of his forelegs and teeth.

175

Aware of the danger in the stallion's restlessness, Henry wanted to warn her. Yet he was afraid to speak lest his voice might upset the Black still more. He waited, fearing a furious kick that would break her ribs, stave in her chest, batter her face.

The Black sniffed the air. His eyes quivered. He swung his head toward Pam, undecided, uneasy. He continued pawing the ground and snorting with impatience, but he did not strike out or move away.

Pam stroked his muzzle with one hand while putting the other over his left eye. Her gaze met Alec's and she nodded to him. He quickly cupped his hands. She was on the stallion's back in a single flowing movement, every joint and muscle from ankle to neck acting as one.

"Okay, Alec," Pam said, "turn him loose."

The Black tossed his head and tried to unseat her. She stayed in the saddle, her hands and seat firm.

Henry expected the Black to erupt with a stranger on his back. If he got away with it now, he would in the race as well. But the Black made no further attempt to unseat Pam. Henry watched her ride off, slim, collected and very proud; he saw no childishness in her face, only strength and resolution. For the moment, he decided, she had made it.

The Black went forward with a long, quick, clean-cut pace. Then, as he went through the gap in the fence, he quickened stride. The stands loomed on the far side of the track, a hovering bulk of steel and concrete and emptiness. Even without the tumult of the crowd or band music, he became excited. He flared his nostrils as he would have done in racing air.

"Easy," Pam said, when he broke into a run. There was no easiness in her own body as she sought control. She must not be just a passenger on his back, not if she intended to race him on Saturday. Alec and Henry were watching. She must be in charge.

The Black had no equal in strength as well as in speed. He wanted to be free of all restraint. His muscled neck was tense and his ears lay back as though the wind of his speed was already whipping past them.

Pam's hands did not yield to him as he asked for more rein. She leaned over his neck and told him to wait. Her eyes were almost closed and her skin was drawn tight about her high, jutting cheekbones. She listened to the sound of his teeth against the steel bit.

Going around the far turn, she cautioned herself, "Not too tight a hold. Don't fight him. Ask him. There, that's better."

The Black went into the homsestretch under control, as Alec and Henry wanted. Pam's world had never looked so beautiful as it did just then, riding the champion past tier upon tier of empty stands. It made no difference to her that nobody was there to watch.

She loosened rein and thrust her knees into his sides, going under the finish wire. At the same instant she called, "Go!"

In spite of the strength of the Black's rush, the shock of his leap, she held on. It was comparable to nothing she'd

177

ever known before, the fury of his run coming with the first stride. Almost before his hoofs struck the packed dirt of the track, he leaped again, throwing her high upon his neck. Her legs saved her from falling and she regained her balance, sitting firm in her seat, and shortening rein.

The Black's speed could not be checked by her snug hold, and his strides became less a racing run than flight itself. His great body stretched in the air, touching ground only to leave it again in a single strike of his hoofs.

Pam's blood caught fire. She released her hold on his mouth. Never had she known anything like it, a furious, magnificent soaring flight! She pressed her face hard against his neck, her body light, almost fluid like his. She was one with him, flying with him, and she had no wish but to soar forever, wherever he would take her.

Coming off the first turn, Pam saw Alec and Henry in the distance and shortened rein. The Black didn't take kindly to the sudden hold on his mouth but he responded by slowing his strides. She had found that with all his great speed and strength, the Black was no wild-eyed monster grabbing the bit and rushing headlong around the track. He would respond to the reins if his rider was strong enough to handle him.

But Pam's arms were beginning to ache from his tremendous pull. The Black took an inch more rein from her and lengthened stride. The inner rail became only a blur, her eyes dimmed by the rush of the wind; his black mane whipped her face, stinging her flesh, hurting her.

A growing numbness came to her arms, weakening her hold on him. Yet her voice was strong as she called repeatedly in his leveled ears, "Easy . . . easy . . ."

The reins slipped again, and the black stallion thundered on. He had the steel bit hard against the bars of his mouth and his incredible speed mounted as he began digging into the track still more.

The furlong poles sped by. Alec and Henry were only blurred images as Pam swept past. She leaned her body with the stallion's as he whipped around the turn and entered the homestretch again.

Ignoring the shooting pains in her arms, she guided him away from the rail and more to the center of the track. She could not check his speed but she could direct it where she wanted; it was like aiming a rifle and sending a bullet speeding on its mark.

The Black raced down the homestretch without needing the roar of a crowd to urge him on. The emptiness of the stands echoed to the rapid beat of his hoofs. He swept past the finish pole, running for the love of running, and Pam rode him for no other reason than to share that love.

Going into the first turn again, the Black slowed of his own accord and Pam threw both arms around his neck and pressed her face against him.

Henry had watched in total silence as the stallion's speed had increased to an almost impossible level. He had never seen the Black go so fast and he believed it was

179

because of the girl's weight, the lightness of a quail. But her balance, too, had been precisely, delicately right for the stallion's greatest freedom and speed. She had been able to check him some, if not rate him as she should, and she'd been able to guide him, direct his tumultuous charge.

"What do you think?" Alec asked, his voice choked with concern, and almost willing to abide by Henry's decision. He didn't want Pam hurt.

Henry did not take his eyes from Pam as she rode the Black toward them. "I've never seen him go any faster," he said finally. "I guess . . . if you want to take the gamble and she does too . . ."

"I don't think there's any doubt how she'll feel about it," Alec said.

"Good," Henry said quietly, "then it's all right with me."

"I'm not sure how good it is," Alec answered.

23 • Dark Saturday

From the beginning there was an air of unreality to Saturday's race. The day was dark, dismal and dripping as the call to the post sounded and the horses and riders came onto the track for the running of the Empire State Handicap. At times they were unrecognizable in the rain-shrouded gloom, emerging eerily from the wispy mist.

Henry pushed his way through the swarming crowd standing before the grandstand despite the drizzling rain. He worked his way toward the middle of the cement apron, realizing it would have been much easier to have watched the race from the press booth. But he didn't want to go up there today. For some reason he wanted to be alone, and the swirling crowd afforded him the most privacy. He didn't want to see the whole race, just the end when it was all over. Why only that? Was he afraid? Of what? For Pam or for himself?

He felt the increased beat of his heart as he listened to the announcer's voice over the loudspeakers, introducing the horses in the feature race. The field was turning in front of the clubhouse and coming back at a canter. He caught a glimpse of the Black, the fifth horse in the field of eight. Alec, riding Napoleon, accompanied the stallion and had a firm hold on his bridle. Pam sat very still on the Black, so small that she hardly seemed to be there at all in the murky light.

"Good luck," he had wished her in the paddock, and he'd meant it. With the day what it was and the track deep in slop, she would need all the racing luck coming to her.

He was aware of the hush that fell over the huge throng as Pam's name was given as the Black's rider. The announcement was followed by loud cheering mixed with cat-calls and boos, and a hum of comments regarding girl riders, some good-natured, some not.

Henry's gaze took in the crowd around him, aware of a restless undercurrent, a feeling of fearful anticipation of what might happen. He was responsible for Pam's being out there. He could have convinced Alec it wasn't safe for her to race.

182

Suddenly Henry felt nausea sweep over him. What had he done? Why had he allowed it? The fact that Alec had wanted her to ride was no excuse. He was older. *He should have known better.*

Now it was too late, much too late. Only the waiting was left, and the minutes would pass intolerably for him. He shoved his way through the crowd, hauling, pulling, determined to reach the rail. "I shouldn't have allowed it," he told himself angrily. "She's only a kid, a little kid. I've been a fool . . . an *old* fool."

The starting gate loomed before Alec like a rain-cloaked monster. Suddenly, Napoleon almost toppled beneath him as the Black swerved hard against the gelding. Alec steadied Napoleon, then his eyes turned to Pam to see how she had taken the jolt. She sat straight in her saddle, gazing neither to the left nor the right, her eyes on the track between the Black's pricked ears.

Alec said nothing; the time for talking was over. Napoleon continued plodding along, doing his job of rebuffing the Black's bumps and never giving an inch.

Over the loudspeakers came the announcement, *"The horses are nearing the starting gate."*

They went behind the gate but continued toward the top of the stretch, the Black cantering easily. Alec watched his horse's long, sure strides in the mud, noting the quiet smooth rhythm, looking him over for the final time, trying to make certain as best he could that everything was as it should be. He had put on the stallion's

183

bridle himself, adjusting it with care. He had made sure the saddle was on right and the lead pad secure, so there would be no sliding backward or forward. He could find nothing wrong. The Black's legs skimmed the track and his long tail waved behind.

The rain glistened on wet racing silks as hoofs splashed through the mud to either side of them. It was like an underwater ballet with colored silks bobbing past to fade in the mist and disappear altogether on the far turn. The Black tried to get away, but Alec held onto his bridle.

It was nearing post time when Alec turned the Black and led him back toward the open doors of the starting gate. The huge stands loomed to his right like an enormous mountain in the dusk.

Aqueduct fans knew all kind of weather, he thought. They were resourceful people, well provided with raincoats and umbrellas. Despite the dismal day, they were safe and secure on the other side of the rail. They had nothing to fear from a sloppy track. It was a far different world on this side. Alec looked at the curtain of rain that wreathed the oval track. The start was midway in the homestretch and the distance to be run one mile and a quarter.

A familiar crewman came walking toward them, his rubber boots squishing in the mud. Turning over the Black to him, Alec said, "Go easy with him, John. He's got someone new in the saddle."

"I know, Alec. Don't worry none."

Alec glanced at Pam. His job was done and the rest was

up to her. The Black was in her hands. He watched her pull down the protective helmet more securely on her head. It was an instinctive movement and he did not believe she was thinking of her accident or the dangerous ride before her. She seemed to be conscious only of the Black, rubbing him between the shoulder blades to comfort him and talking all the while, unaware of anyone else, including himself. Her face looked grim but there was a relaxed calmness to her body that comforted him a little.

He supposed she felt as he did when the waiting was over and the race at hand.

"Lots of luck, Pam," he said.

She didn't answer but he saw the slight quivers at the corners of her mouth as she tried to smile.

The official starter, standing on his platform just ahead and to the left of the gate, said, "Don't bring up that Number Five horse too fast, John. No hurry. Wait for the others."

The starter didn't want any mistakes in this race. A bad start could ruin his day. His sagging, grim face betrayed the softness of his voice and his patient instructions to his ground crew. He was an amiable man, of even temperament, as a man must be to have survived fifty years of starting races. Once the horses were in the gate and gone, his job would be finished until the next race. But this was the Empire State Handicap, worth over $100,000, and some eighty thousand people were there to watch it.

He glanced at the girl up on Number 5. He had never thought he'd see anyone but Alec Ramsay up on the Black. It was bound to make his job tougher.

He had eight good men working in his ground crew, one for every horse in the race. Each man knew his job and the quirks of every horse. He kept a book on the gate peculiarities of almost every horse racing at Aqueduct and there were more than two thousand of them. He glanced at his program to confirm his notes on this field. No slips today, not in the gate anyway.

The starter was well aware of the television cameras just off the track, focused on the horses as they approached the gate. It wasn't like the old days when his men carried a switch in one pocket, a rope in another and a bull whip around their necks. Then he could say anything he wanted to the riders without being hauled before the track stewards or even into court. Now everyone knew what went on in the gate, including millions of television viewers.

"Okay, it's time," he called to his ground crew. "Bring up that Number One horse, Woody. Keep his head up. He likes to get it down, you know. That's it. Bring him forward now. Good boy." Dark Legend was safely in his stall.

Sun Dancer was next. "George, you won't have trouble with that Number Two horse if you walk in front of him. Go right into his stall ahead of him. That's it." Here was another girl rider, Becky Moore, and he recalled what had happened the last time these two girls had been in

186

the same race. Well, he'd better forget it. What happened *after* the race began wasn't part of his job. "Next horse," he called.

This horse would give him trouble if he wasn't careful. "Sid," he said, "remember you've got to back that Number Three horse in! Come around to the front and start all over again." He waited patiently as Artless was brought to the front of the gate and carefully backed into his stall, fighting every step of the way.

"Hold his tail up, Sid, so he won't rear on you! That's it. Now you've got him. Stay there until he settles down."

The starter turned his gaze to the Number 4 horse. No trouble here. Challenger walked into his stall without a fuss.

Now for the big horse, Number 5. "Easy with him, John," he called, "very, very easy. Hand on his bridle *lightly*. Don't force him one step. Walk to his side, well to his side. Ramsay, help move him up now . . . I mean . . ." He'd forgotten the girl's name and looked at his program. When he turned back, the Black was in his stall, standing straight and still, with the girl leaning forward, talking to him. Maybe she wouldn't have trouble after all, he decided. He had to admit that she had a lot of courage to be riding the Black. He called for the next horse.

Sword Master was sluggish; he looked half-asleep. "Shake up that Number Six horse, Cliff. He needs prodding. Give him one. Yeah, that's it." Sword Master went

187

quietly into his stall.

The Number 7 horse followed quickly, his handler having no trouble with him. "That's the way to do it," the starter called. Royal Pharaoh was in his stall, and there was only one more horse to go.

The starter turned to the Number 8 stall, making certain that the front door had been left open. It was well known that Gallant Teddy wouldn't enter a closed stall. "Okay, bring him in now, Bill," he ordered his crewman. "Grab his ear to keep his attention until you get him inside. Fine, that's the way to do it. Now, close both doors. Easy. Good. That's it. Okay, we're all set."

His gaze swept down the row of closed stalls. It was a good field, no problems other than the usual. But there was lots of tension in a race of this importance. The jockeys were keyed up and the horses sensed it.

The starter glanced at their faces, wet with rain, making certain each rider was well balanced in his seat and ready to go. Willy Watts was young in age but old in experience; he seemed as nervous as Becky Moore, who sat on Sun Dancer in the next stall. Sam Dillon was grim-faced, a veteran rider, old in experience with over six thousand winners to his credit, making him the second best jockey of all time. Tommy Ryan, winner of the Kentucky Derby this year, was having his hands full with Gallant Teddy, who was as full of fight as he had ever known him to be.

"Bill," the starter called, "give Ryan a hand with that Number Eight horse. Tail him. Get it over the side of the stall. Keep him still or we'll never get out of here."

Time was ticking away and the starter turned back to the Number 8 horse with anxious eyes, knowing it was already two minutes past post time. He bit his lip, recalling other races, other years when he'd had bad starts in important races. He mustn't let it happen this time to mar his record. He'd wait as long as necessary to get a good start.

Gallant Teddy continued plunging despite the crewman and the jockey's efforts to hold him down. He half-reared and twisted as he came down, almost unseating his rider. Then, suddenly, he plunged forward to break through the door and was running down the track with the red-coated marshal alertly cutting him off before he had gone very far. But it meant more time, waiting for him to come back.

The horses in the stalls had settled down as if they knew the break was not coming immediately. An indication of how smart they were today, the starter thought. They stood there like old cows, waiting for Gallant Teddy to return.

Back in his stall, Gallant Teddy continued fighting both handler and rider. He backed up and tried to pin the jockey against the side of the stall. Tommy Ryan looked scared. He had every right to be, the starter thought. Ryan had been out of action for almost a year after breaking his leg in a fall at Belmont.

Finally, with the help of extra handlers, they got Gallant Teddy straight in his stall and still. The starter got ready to push the button that would open the doors. He'd wait another few seconds, giving Gallant Teddy a chance to settle down a little more.

The break was coming and the horses knew it. Sun Dancer struck out a foreleg in eagerness. Challenger twisted slightly in his stall. The Black shifted uneasily, his feet dancing, pawing. The starter kept his eyes on him. He'd been expecting it all along. The Black was a "bitter" horse, one that got mean and tough at the ringing of the bell. He hoped the girl knew what to do once he turned them loose.

"Steady now," the starter called to the riders. "I'm not sending you away until every single one of you is quiet. I don't care how long it takes." Yet his finger played with the button in his hand, touching it lightly, ready to push.

24 • *The Empire State Handicap*

Having left Napoleon with Deb, Alec hurried through the throng in front of the grandstand. He wanted to be able to see the whole oval; he didn't want to miss one stride the Black took today. Where should he go? He had to make up his mind in a hurry.

The stands and cement apron were black with people, black as the rain that was weeping from the sky. Only the track was clear, a wet sloppy road soon to be filled. Overhead he could hear seagulls flying and calling. The planes at Kennedy Airport were grounded but not the birds. Their sad cries drifted down to him, saddened by the mist. Listening to them, he felt isolated, preyed upon by his fears for Pam.

He saw Henry near the finish line, but he didn't want to be with him today. Neither did he want to go upstairs to the crowded press section. He wanted to watch the race without listening to the emotional outbursts of others.

Anxiously, he turned back to the starting gate. Gallant Teddy was giving his rider and handlers a lot of trouble. The delay afforded him more time, but he must decide quickly where to go.

Over the loudspeakers came the clipped, cultured voice of racing's most famous announcer, *"It is now post time."*

Alec glanced up at the announcer's lonely booth high on top of the grandstand. Yes, he decided, that is where he would go. He would be welcome there, providing he kept absolutely quiet during the calling of the race. There would be no dramatics or emotionalism in that soundproofed workshop, no editorializing or guessing, no partiality or faking—only precise, accurate, objective, split-second calling of the race from start to finish.

Alec hurried toward the grandstand, hunching his shoulders against the rain and the people who jostled him. Inside the lower lobby he ran across the vast, open area toward a special door. Reaching it, he nodded to a track policeman, showed his pass and stepped through. He raced down a long corridor and stopped before the private elevator that would take him quickly to the top tier of the grandstand. He pressed the button and impatiently waited for the elevator to arrive, knowing he had less than a minute to get there.

The door opened and he stepped inside, pushing the top button urgently and willing the door to close. Quietly, the elevator left the ground floor and began rising.

Alec leaned back against the side of the elevator, his whole body suddenly shaking, his legs throbbing and feeling like balloons. He had difficulty controlling the thoughts that flickered through his mind as the elevator rose, then stopped, and the door opened.

She had no right to be out there. He recognized it, accepted it now, when it was too late. She was independent, headstrong, destined for a tragic end. What was she doing in a race against professionals, hardened in mind and feelings, when she should be walking on grass in her bare feet? Yet he knew she would have had it no other way. She would ride this race as she did everything else— with an overwhelming zest to experience whatever life had to offer.

Reaching the door of the announcer's booth, Alec knocked before going inside. The man standing alone in the glass-fronted room was short and chunky, not altogether befitting his heroic stature as the greatest racetrack caller of all time. His lively brown eyes under bushy eyebrows turned to Alec. He pointed toward an extra pair of binoculars lying on the table, then quickly turned back to the track.

For whatever reason the start had been delayed, Alec

193

knew that the extra moments had enabled him to arrive in time to see the whole race. He picked up the binoculars and moved over to the large window. He could see the bank of rain that closed over the oval track like a gigantic tunnel. The backstretch was barely visible in the gloom. It would be a difficult race for the announcer to call.

The great man had the microphone holder around his neck with five mikes attached to it. He raised the binoculars to his eyes, his feet planted firmly on the floor, his balance on his toes, as if he were one with the horses and would break from the gate with them. A second later, in his high-pitched, precise voice, he said, *"They're off!"*

Alec watched the horses break from the gate. Artless and Dark Legend broke first and went immediately to the front, clear of trouble. Sun Dancer was squeezed by Challenger, who swerved sharply and brushed the rail. Sword Master bore out, taking the Black with him. Royal Pharaoh slipped and lost his running action. Gallant Teddy was sluggish getting away, then came alive, bolting for the outside rail before his rider got him aimed down the stretch and running.

The Black was moving effortlessly, despite his being carried out by Sword Master. Alec knew his horse could handle the footing with ease. He urged Pam on, hoping she would break clear of the steel-shod traffic jam, a milling tangle of horses and riders. Gallant Teddy was floundering in the slop and bouncing up and down. Sword Master and Royal Pharaoh were also having trouble getting hold of the track and slipping dangerously. Sword Master skittered and banged into the Black. Alec winced as he watched Pam steady him while keeping her own balance. Luckily, she and the Black had recovered but they had lost ground to Sun Dancer on the rail. Several lengths beyond, Artless had gone in front of Dark Legend.

As the horses flashed by almost directly beneath the booth, the announcer made his first call, speaking in his precise, clipped voice, *"It's Artless by a head over Dark Legend. Sun Dancer is third. Sword Master is fourth. The Black is fifth. Challenger is sixth. Gallant Teddy is seventh and Royal Pharaoh is eighth and last."*

The announcer had separated the horses in the closely packed field by matching their names to silks and blinkers, never to the numbers on their saddle-cloths. He would call each horse by name and position many times in a little over two flashing minutes. He worked in split seconds, accuracy his only goal. Yet as the horses swept by their silks were almost too mud-splattered to be identifiable.

Alec moved closer to the window. He knew the pace being set by Artless and Dark Legend was not as fast as it had been a few seconds ago. Did Pam realize that the two veteran riders were working as a team and skillfully shortening their mounts' strides? It was an old trick and always good when executed with finesse, which was the case now. There was no noticeable slackening of speed by the leaders as they approached the clubhouse turn.

195

But couldn't Pam tell by the Black's mounting fury at being held back?

Artless and Dark Legend could easily go the full distance if the race was run slowly enough. Sun Dancer in third position had the most to gain by the slow pace; Becky Moore had him well placed on the rail and he was a fresh, lightly weighted horse. Sun Dancer would be tough to beat if he was strong at the end when the Black's heavy impost began to tell.

The field, still tightly packed except for the two leaders, swung wide going into the turn, some of them slipping dangerously under the hard drives now being waged by their riders. It was apparent to Alec that the other jockeys realized the pace was too slow, even if Pam didn't, and were going after Artless and Dark Legend. Challenger, racing just inside the Black, skidded as Sam Dillon pushed him to greater speed. Sword Master, too, was under full steam with Mitch West laying on leather. Gallant Teddy was moving up, followed closely by Royal Pharaoh on the outside, their riders too using hands and feet. Pam alone sat still, but Alec saw that the Black was breaking from her restraining hands and lengthening his strides.

Sweeping into the first turn, Alec watched the Black take more rein from Pam. He was dangerously close to Challenger's heaving hindquarters.

The Black's head came down, fighting Pam, but she was successful in shortening his strides so he did not run over the horse in front of him. He swerved abruptly to the inside, almost unseating her, and took off after Sun Dancer, who was now moving on the rail with blistering speed.

The Black's head came down again, indicating his resentment of the hold Pam had on him. He wanted to run all out and was telling her so forcefully. Alec knew well the terrible pull she was experiencing in her arms.

Over the loudspeakers the announcer's voice had become high-pitched even though it remained eloquent and precise, *"That's Artless still in front by a length. Dark Legend is second by a head over Sun Dancer coming fast on the rail. Challenger and Sword Master are neck and neck on the outside. The Black is sixth. Gallant Teddy is seventh. Royal Pharaoh is eighth.*

Alec listened to the call but his eyes remained on the Black and Pam. He realized that even if he were in the saddle he would be having a rough time with his horse. Like human beings, horses had their good days and bad days, and this was one of the Black's worst. He wanted no waiting, no resting; neither could he be placed where Pam thought it would be safer for him to race. The Black was racing as he had in the early days, when he was strictly a come-from-behind horse, and it had taken a lot of racing luck as well as tremendous speed to break through large fields to win. For Alec, as it must now be for Pam, it had been the most dangerous time of all.

Alec knew she was trying to guide the Black away from where he wanted to go, *right up on the heels of Sun Dancer!* Pam had her hands full and, for a few seconds, the Black refused to respond. Then he relented, his strides turning to the outside and lengthening, his hoofs scarcely touching the ground. Alec watched him draw alongside Challenger, fearful of what he might do.

Somehow, Pam managed to hold him off Challenger. But the Black was taking out his anger and frustration on her arms. Alec wondered how she was able to stand the pull.

Now Dark Legend was directly in his path. Sun Dancer was to his left and a little to the front, behind Artless. None of the horses or riders on his right gave way. The Black took more rein and Alec knew Pam would not be able to control him much longer.

They reached the middle of the turn with the Black racing Challenger stride for stride. He was pinned and trapped with no place to go. He had no choice but to shorten his strides or go down when he ran over Dark Legend's heels.

The announcer placed a moist hand on a paper towel and pressed it, drying his hand. He could no longer separate the horses to call their positions accurately. They were a pounding line stretched across the track. Their silks were indistinguishable. He could only guess at their positions and he would do no faking. He remained silent.

Alec saw Pam try to avoid a collision with Dark Legend. But her pull on the reins only shattered whatever patience the stallion had left. Angered beyond all control, he twisted his head and body to free himself of rein and bit and hands. Pam swung with him, trying to stay in the saddle. The Black plunged forward again and the force of it sent her onto his neck, her hands seeking a hold in his mane. She lurched with him, going forward then backward in the saddle.

Watching her, Alec put his hands against the window sill to steady himself. He saw Pam regain her seat, but the Black was now completely out of control. There was no telling what he would do in the backstretch or, more important, what would happen to Pam because of it. Alec rubbed his eyes, his sight blurred.

The Black came off the turn and the backstretch rail slipped by faster and faster. There were no hands to slow him down. He was free, his neck stretched out and ears flat against his head. He raced after the others with Pam only a passenger on his back.

Artless, laboring in front, began slowing and his jockey went for his whip. It came hissing down with brutal suddenness, but the blow acted as a brake instead of achieving more speed. He stopped so short that his hoofs might have plunged right down into the earth. Becky Moore avoided his heels by inches and sent Sun Dancer into the lead.

The Black caught the field, and Alec was fearful of what might happen when he plunged into the tangled mass of horses in his path. He saw Pam trying to guide him, if not stop him, but it was futile. Her arms would be torn from their sockets by the force of the stallion's charge!

The Black tipped Dark Legend's heels, and almost

199

went down. He recovered quickly to hurl himself into a narrow gap between Challenger and Sword Master.

Alec remained deathly still, knowing that just one false step and the Black and Pam would go down beneath the hoofs of the field. But suddenly the Black had cut his way through, bursting out of the pack, stretched low over the ground, still in a shattering charge. And only Sun Dancer was ahead of him!

The announcer made his call, filling his lungs and projecting his voice to its greatest volume. *"Going into the far turn it's Sun Dancer in front by a length over the Black. Sword Master is third. Gallant Teddy is fourth. Challenger is fifth. Royal Pharaoh is sixth. Dark Legend is seventh. Artless is last."*

Alec moved his binoculars to Sun Dancer, and he saw Becky glance back at Pam, then go for her whip. Sun Dancer was not a spent horse and his sustained drive under Becky's whip continued around the turn. The Black's speed took him too wide and he lost ground to Sun Dancer, racing hard on the rail.

They entered the homestretch, the great stands looming on their right, the crowd on its feet. Pam was sitting still in her saddle but Becky Moore was riding as if her life depended upon it, using hands and feet and whip.

Watching closely, Alec rode with Pam every step of the way. He knew the Black's heavy impost was beginning to tell. The dead leaden weights and his rebellious fury had taken their toll. Much of his speed and stamina had been wrung out of him.

Alec saw too that Sun Dancer, driven beyond his natural powers by Becky's violent riding, was surpassing himself, taking almost impossible strides that matched the Black's. All Becky needed to do was to hold him there to win. Her determination to beat the champion was carrying Sun Dancer along, raising him, working a miracle upon him so he was capable of astonishing effort. An effort that, in the end, Alec knew, would leave him a broken and empty horse. But it was victory *now* that Becky wanted, tomorrow didn't matter.

The cries from the crowd rose to shattering heights as the challenger fought back the champion and kept his lead. Becky Moore's whip rose and fell on Sun Dancer's haunches. He responded to her beating by quickening his strides with less than a furlong to go.

Alec clenched his fists and pounded them against the window sill. His throat was constricted, his jaws glued together. His eyes never left the bobbing heads coming toward him. Sun Dancer was hanging on doggedly under Becky's grueling, punishing drive. He was being asked for more than he had to give. He had to crack under the pace. He couldn't last. Or could he?

In the final strides of the race, Alec recalled Pam's most important stake in it—the memory of a colt who would still be alive had it not been for the same kind of ruthless riding. And now Pam was out to beat Becky not through violence but on her own terms and in her own way, the only way she knew, by being one with her horse and *asking* for everything he had to give without unnecessary punishment.

The Black's breathing was coming hard, Alec knew;

air as well as ground was running out on him. Pam continued to sit very still, never touching him with her hands or legs, and Alec loved her all the more for knowing his horse was giving all he had.

Watching them come down to the finish wire, Alec saw Pam shift her weight on the stallion's back as if she hoped to carry him forward by her own light body and strength. Incredible as it seemed, the Black responded to her shift in balance, and Alec yelled at the top of his voice. His cry came over the loudspeakers, amplified a thousand times, yet it was lost in the tremendous roar already rising from the stands.

The Black had forged alongside Sun Dancer in one magnificent stride and the leader suddenly gave way, his strides faltering under the Black's challenge and the flogging whip of his rider.

The fans watched the Black go under the wire, their applause stilled by his flying image. Even in the day's semi-darkness his brilliance as champion was brighter than ever before. He had proved his greatness again, this time with a stranger on his back.

25 ◆ *The Wind Her Fingers*

They left Aqueduct for the farm soon after the race, with Alec driving Pam's car, resplendent in its painted flowers.

"Henry's changed," Alec told Pam. "He wants you to stay very much. He won't hire Mike Costello or anyone else."

"I'm glad he's changed his mind about having girls around," she said.

"It's not just that," Alec explained. "I think Henry's found that he's not too old to change his mind about a lot of things. I think he's going to be more understanding of others even if their standards are different from his own."

"That's great," she said, "really great." Pam paused, thoughtful, and then added, "But he was right about one thing. I learned what human frailty is today. I was scared out there."

"But you rode as if you weren't," Alec said. "That's what's important." His eyes left the traffic ahead to glance her way. "No one in this world could have ridden the Black as you did today."

"No one else would have had the chance," she said, turning to him. "I know that as well as you do, Alec. I knew it when I asked you to let me ride him. Letting me have the Black was the greatest thing you could have done for anyone."

"You're not just anyone," he said. "I love you."

"And I love you," she said. "More now than ever because I know what you gave up for me."

"But, still, you won't stay?"

"I want to but I can't," she said miserably.

Alec drove in silence, knowing he could do nothing more to change her mind. He must accept the fact that their being together was not going to last. He had tried everything but her decision to leave was unshakable. Moreover, he had his pride. He didn't want to plead with her like a slavering puppy. The decision had to come from her if it was to be any good between them. Despite his knowing this, he found himself nose-diving into a black pit of depression and fought against it. He wanted no bloody battles with himself or with Pam, loving her as he did. She loved him, he believed, but she loved life more. She was a wanderer, chasing the sun wherever it might lead in search of new experiences and challenges.

"What are you thinking about?" she asked.

"Nothing but beautiful thoughts," he said bitterly.

She twisted her head to look at him. "Hell is more likely from your eyes," she said. "I don't mean to be cruel."

"How do you expect me to feel?" he asked. He felt the tightness in his stomach, swelling, plunging, and sought to stop it by saying angrily, "There's no magical power in frustration, Pam, and that's how I feel about us."

"Frustration?" she repeated. "I thought we had something else, such as being true to one's self and to each other—real happiness."

"All right," he said quietly. "I'm going to spoil our happiness by saying 'I love you too much to let you go.'"

"But you *must,*" she said as quietly.

"Why?"

"Because I think we may both get what we want in time," she said, her voice trembling and very close to tears. "But not now. I'm not ready to settle down any more than you are. I've too many things to see and do, and so have you. It wouldn't be fair to either of us. We'd feel trapped, unable to do what we want to do."

"Will it be any better later on?" Alec asked, trying

205

to keep the bitterness from his voice.

"I think so," she said softly. "That's what I meant when I said we'll both get what we want in time. It shouldn't be frustrating, this waiting—not with all the things we have to do—and if you love me as I love you." She paused before going on. "Look at it this way, Alec. If I asked *you* to leave, would you come with *me?*"

Alec kept his gaze on the road but he knew her eyes were questioning him as well as her voice.

"No," he said finally. "You know I wouldn't. I couldn't. Racing is where I belong."

He heard her laugh but knew there was no laughter in her eyes, no more than in his own.

"So there," she said. "It's as simple as that. You have important things to do and so have I."

"But there's a difference," he said. "At the farm you'd be close to nature and all that you love."

"I know," she answered, "and I want to come back to it and to you. But not *now*," she added hastily. "It's too early for both of us."

"You'll be hurt, if you go on as you do," Alec said. "They're going to knock you down. You'll find people who are lots worse than Henry, and you won't be able to change them as you did him."

"Then, when I come back, we'll help to outbreed them," she said gayly. "Don't worry so."

"I'm not going to wait until you come back," Alec said. "I'm coming after you. Every place you go, I'll be there, if only for a day at a time, until I find you're ready

206

to come back to stay. I'm *not* giving you up."

"That will be best of all," she answered.

Reaching the farm, he waited in the apartment while she packed. And all the time the phonograph played, for she left it until last. The music crashed like thunder in the small room. Somewhere in those clanging chords, somewhere in those ferocious guitars, somewhere in those unintelligible choruses he sensed a clue to her *need* to go. But he couldn't find it. The music was too loud, too primitive. It rent his stomach and his mind.

Only when she played records sung by the folk singers did he find a message in the music. He listened to the clear beauty of their voices and lyrics as they sang sweetly of love and joy and morning sunshine; that was the Pam he knew.

"Where are you going?" he asked, finally, knowing he could do no more than to ask the direction her path would take.

She emerged from behind the kitchen screen where she had changed from city clothes. She wore a floppy cowboy hat and her standard uniform of jeans, a faded blue shirt with button-down collar that had belonged to her father, and brown loafers in need of a good saddle-soaping. As clean as she kept the stable tack, she seemed to take great pride in never touching her loafers with the sponge. He wondered at the contradiction. Perhaps it was that she didn't attach much importance to her own appearance and, if anything, played it down.

"I'm going to visit a friend in Maryland," she said; then aware of his suspicions added, ". . . a *girl* friend, Alec, an old school friend. I'll give you her name and address."

"But must you go tonight?"

"I like driving at night and Nancy's expecting me." She paused, looking at him intently. "I'm not changing my mind, Alec, so please don't change yours."

She went on with her packing and Alec carried the cardboard boxes down to the car as she filled them. They often touched in the transfer, and the contact was almost like an animal form of communication with no need for words to express their feelings for each other.

When darkness came she didn't put on the lights. "That's it," she said, "all done." Slinging her black-leather shoulder bag over her arm, she stood before him.

He could see her face in the light from the doorway; she seemed so young, so open—too open. He felt much older than she, as old as Henry. Was it that they belonged to different ages—hers one of trust while he had been brought up in an age of cynicism? She would continue to lead the life that made sense to her. She was doing her own thing in her own time.

"I wish you'd put off leaving until tomorrow," he persisted. "You're tired, and it could be dangerous driving all the way to Maryland. It'll take you most of the night."

"I like driving to meet the dawn," she said.

He knew there would be no changing her mind, that she would go to Maryland and beyond as she and her fate saw fit. It made no difference that her paths, like the night before her, would be dark.

She put her arms around him, and said, "I'll be expecting you wherever I am, just like you said."

"You'll always let me know where you are?"

"Always."

The taste of her skin against his own, the warmth of her breath and the sound of her voice stirred emotions that went deeper than any he had ever known. How could he let her go?

He kissed her and held her closer still. "I'll come with you," he said. "We'll get married tonight."

She pushed her head away from his, and something within him collapsed as he looked into her eyes.

"You'd soon hate me for taking you away," she answered. "Don't you understand what I mean, Alec? . . . what I've tried to say before? *I'm* not ready for marriage even if you think you are. And I think too much of marriage not to be ready for it. It's the greatest challenge I'll ever know, and I want to make it work. I want to have more to give you than I can give you now. Please, Alec," she pleaded, "don't let me change my mind. Let me grow up a little more."

His arms dropped from her, and he turned his head away. "It's no good, Pam," he said angrily. "Your world is halfway between imagination and reality. Don't you see? It sets you adrift, seeking what it ought to be, might be, yet can *never* be. It can only become a nightmare for you!"

When he had finished, she swung the leather bag over her shoulder and left the apartment without looking back. He followed, already regretting his outburst, knowing her rejection of him was responsible for it. Yet he meant what he'd said. He was no different from others, young and old, who doubted that anything could be changed from the way it was, and who believed that anyone who tried was not only a fool but could be hurt terribly. He was fearful for Pam's very life and, loving her as he did, he had needed to speak out.

Below, she went from one stall to the next, saying good-by to the two-year-olds she had trained. He followed in silence, speaking only when she reached Black Sand's empty stall.

"Would you like to see where I buried him?"

"No," she answered without taking her eyes from the stall. "I don't think of him as being there anyway. He's with me as I am with him. We'll be together always."

"We brought up another colt for training," Alec said, hoping to interest her. "You'd like him, Pam. His name's Blackjack, and he's the only colt we have who's sired by the Black. He's in the paddock outside. You can see him as you leave. Maybe you'll like him enough to . . ."

She laughed as she turned to him, and he was glad that she was no longer angry.

"No maybes," she replied. "We've both said what we've had to say."

"But . . ."

"No buts either," she said adamantly, taking his arm

210

and moving him toward the door. "I'm going now."

"I was going to tell you that the Black's coming home," he said. "I was saving it as a surprise if you stayed."

"Then you're retiring him? I'm glad, Alec."

He looked into her eyes, knowing his answer was important to her. She was as concerned for his safety as he was for hers. She really wanted to find out if he and the Black were going on in that steel-shod world she'd known today.

"He'll get a good rest but I'm not retiring him, Pam," Alec said. "He's a race horse, not a loafer. Don't think for a moment he'd have a great life, standing here. He wouldn't. He'd miss racing. He'd miss the cheering and all that goes with it. He wouldn't like it around here, Pam, not for long, anyway. He needs to go."

"You mean like me," she said quietly.

In her face he saw a trace of humor and a wrinkle at the corners of her mouth, a wandering look. "Like you," he agreed sadly, putting his arms around her.

She got into the old car, her hand on his through the window. "Here's my friend's address in Maryland," she said. "I'll be there two weeks."

"Then where?" he asked, wanting to know so he could find her again if anything kept him from seeing her in Maryland.

"I'm going to France," she said.

"France," he repeated. "You're kidding."

His astonishment seemed to amuse her and she smiled

211

"No, I mean it," she said seriously. "I'm going to work in Paris for a while, until I get enough money saved for a trip somewhere else. Maybe Switzerland. I've always wanted to ski. I can water-ski, but that's a lot different, I guess. Then I'd like to go to Vienna to see the Lipizzan horses at the Spanish Riding School. Maybe I can even get a job there. I want to go to Ireland, too," she went on eagerly. "I've read so much about their hunts and stee-plechases. Have you ever jumped, Alec?"

"No," he said, overwhelmed by her itinerary. He intended to go after her as soon as the Black came home for a rest, but it was not going to be easy for him. France and Switzerland, Austria and Ireland were a long way off.

"Well, when we're in Ireland we'll learn to jump to-gether," she said.

Alec said nothing but he didn't let go of her hand. He felt her fingers clutch his, and for a moment he thought she might get out of the car and stay. Then quickly she shifted into first, the gears grinding and making a hor-rible sound.

"You should get that transmission fixed," he said. "If you wait, we'll get to it the first thing in the morning."

"Don't worry," she called, moving away. "Every-thing will go smoothly."

"I'll be down to Maryland," he shouted after her.

He caught a last glimpse of her face beneath the floppy cowboy hat. Her mouth held a queer smile as if she had looked into the future and knew what would happen. Her final words reached him, carried on the wind as free as she. "I'll look for you, Alec. I love you. . . . Remember, I love you."

The new colt, Blackjack, stopped grazing as the car went past. Then he began following it, running along the fence with majestic, unrestrained power. Watching him, Alec thought of the black riderless horse that symbolized a lost leader in the ancient days of mounted warriors, a sign that his master had fallen and would ride no more.

Alec's eyes left the horse to follow the red rear lights of the car as it turned down the highway. Pam had not fallen but was going on to other adventures. He wouldn't let her get away. He would follow no matter where she went until, finally, the day would come when she'd return with him to Hopeful Farm, and they would be together always.

Alec climbed the fence and walked across the paddock. He would make sure his days were well occupied until he saw Pam again. He would plunge into his work and many hours would pass without his thinking of her. But there would be times when his thoughts of her would escape and run rampant, especially at night; when he would walk the fields, knowing he would not find what he was looking for. He might be able to think of all sorts of remedies but there was no chance of amputating the past completely until Pam walked at his side again.

Alec came to a stop when Blackjack saw him. The colt would be a good one, just as he'd told Pam, being over

213

sixteen hands and sired by the Black. He decided he would ride him in the morning, early, before anyone else was up. Afterward, he would return to Aqueduct and join the rest of the world, as Pam had done.

Blackjack came over to him hesitantly, unsure of himself and of Alec. He stopped a short distance away, his eyes large and bright in the starshine.

Alec waited for him to come all the way, making no move, not hurrying him at all. He felt a new sense of patience, of sureness, of rightness. It was real and here to stay. It was the result of his love for Pam and for what she had taught him. She had softness yet resilience, gaiety yet earnestness, a need for solitude yet an outpouring of love for her fellow man and, most of all, she had faith in a beloved world. She had touched him with her magic and he hoped that in some way he had returned the gift.

A soft breeze swept his face, and his eyes turned to the star-lit heavens. Whenever he wasn't with her, her fingers would be the wind and the wind her fingers, and all space would be the smile of her.